T0036760

# PRAISE FOR DAVID AGRANOFF

"It's time to face the truth. You've always wanted to see vampires fight World War II Nazis! In your heart, you craved it! But you said, no one could do it right. You hadn't counted on David Agranoff. He's shown us how it's done right. Don't miss the high-concept schaden-freude and fierce plotting of *The Last Night to Kill Nazis!*"
   — **John Shirley**, author of *Stormland*

"At the beginning of *The Last Night to Kill Nazis*, David Agranoff lights a fuse that burns with perfectly-timed suspense to an explosive resolution. This mash-up of World War II thriller and vampire horror is exciting and authentic; like peanut butter and chocolate it shouldn't work, but it does. I loved it!"
   — **Lisa Morton**, six-time Bram Stoker Award-Winner

"The Last Night to Kill Nazis is solid storytelling packed with real history and—if you are of the mindset that evil deserves to be punished—a whole hell of a lot of bloody, gratifying fun."
   — **Alma Katsu**, author of *The Wehrwolf*

"A brutal, bloody rampage, Agranoff has created great characters and daring storytelling. I guarantee you have never had so much fun seeing Nazis meeting their grue-some fates."
   — **Tim Lebbon**, author of *The Silence* and *The Last Storm*

"*The Last Night to Kill Nazis* is a glorious exploration of culpability and trauma. A blood-soaked thrill ride bursting with frenetic energy that recalls the finest of exploitation and action films. David Agranoff looks at the horrors of the second World War with unflinching honesty, exploring a culpability that few other writers dare to. This is a book that balances exceptional depth with absolute fun and terrific characters. Come for Nazis dying horribly, and stay for the fantastic writing."

—**Zachary Rosenberg**, author of *Hungers As Old As This Land* and *The Long Shalom*

"This is high-concept genre fiction, people. Agranoff has performed alchemy on those late-night History Channel documentaries like *The Nazis' Supernatural Weapons* and crossed it with *The A-Team*. This book is a possessed slaughterhouse of language and imagery, running off an engine of righteous anger and revenge. And we should be pleased. I know I am."

—**Kyle Winkler**, author of *The Nothing That Is* and *Boris Says the Words*

"A masterpiece of characterization, pacing, and atmosphere! In *The Last Night to Kill Nazis*, David Agranoff delivers a true page-turner that pits supernatural evil against even darker and more horrifying human evil in a story that hearkens back to the best of the classic World War II and horror movies—yet feels completely relevant today."

—**James Chambers**, Bram Stoker Award-Winning Author of *On the Hierophant Road* and *On the Night Border*.

# THE LAST NIGHT TO KILL NAZIS

### DAVID AGRANOFF

Copyright © 2023 by David Agranoff

ISBN: 9781955904728

Cover by Joel Amat Güell

CLASH Books

Troy, NY

All rights reserved.

This is a work of fiction. Names, characters, businesses, places, events, locales, and incidents are either the products of the author's imagination or used in a fictitious manner. Any resemblance to actual persons, living or dead, or actual events is purely coincidental.

No part of this book may be reproduced in any form or by any electronic or mechanical means, including information storage and retrieval systems, without written permission from the author, except for the use of brief quotations in a book review.

*This novel is dedicated personally to John Shirley, you always inspired me to tell stories that matter, thank you for the advice and friendship. Globally, it is dedicated to those who work to fight fascism. The Struggle is far from over.*

# PROLOGUE

HE PLACED the barrel of the pistol against his temple knowing he was the most hated man in the world. Eva had accepted their fate long ago, that is why they married just a day before. It was symbolic but he owed her that. Together they gave gentle pets to Blondie as she fought for her last breaths. The Shepherd had been by their side in times both good and bad, Eva looked away, she couldn't look into his dying eyes. He knew the Russians wouldn't spare her, if she lived the Russians would delight in her torture, and more importantly, he had to know if the pills were real. She was a good girl one last time.

The dog jerked and died in Eva's arms. Himmler had not betrayed him; his worst fear was that he would close his eyes believing death was here and wake up in a surrender planned by his own men. Thankfully not, he would die before the Russians dug their way into the bunker. Eva had gripped his hand and he knew Blondie was dead as the warmth drained. Even as deep as they were, he heard the Russian march now. They were beating the Americans in the race to Berlin.

A thousand years the Reich was meant to rule and now his armies were gone, he gave orders to units that didn't respond.

In the end, it felt like only Goebbels and Boorman stayed loyal, Adolf did the same for Germany, but he was alone now. If he didn't pull the trigger, the Russians would torture him, the Americans say they want trials but no one believes that for a minute. The bombs that rained down on his cities killed Germans with no discretion.

*That army is coming for you, Adolf. You could have been an artist, you could have died with your father or your mother. You could have died in the Great War. Ypres, Somme, or Arras. Had you just died in the mud like a good soldier you wouldn't be here. You didn't have to speak every time. You didn't need to feel the swelling crowds. You didn't need it.*

The trigger was so close to his finger, he regretted that he swallowed the pill already. He felt woozy, he might lose his grip and not get another chance. He couldn't take any chances. He had to squeeze that...

*Bang.*

Alice jumped. It had been several minutes since anyone spoke. All eyes turned back to the Fuhrer's office. Gerda held the tissue to her face and wept. They all knew it was coming but hearing it in that final moment hurt every inch of her body. There were tears, a soft weeping behind her, she didn't see who it was, as her eyes locked on the door. It was impossible to fathom. She never thought this day would come. Slowly Gerda's hand took hers.

To the German people he was their glorious leader, to Alice and Gerda, he had become more. Gerda worked directly with Boorman typing up matters of state. Alice typed his letters. She typed plenty of letters thanking families for their sacrifices, but her greatest joy was sitting with the Fuhrer as he dictated letters to his soldiers out on the front, or to the youth.

Those were happy moments for the leader. Away from the stress and weight of the nation and world on his shoulders, he was charming with the girls in his secretary pool. Eva was his love, but they were the ones he talked to in order to escape his responsibility. Alice talked to him for many hours over tea, and no matter what happened with the war she wanted to hold on to that. He brought Germany back from the misery of the depression and made the country great again. She loved him for it.

Joseph Goebbels was a gaunt man on his best day and now he was the color of chalk. He walked to the door. His fists tight against his mouth, as if to hold in a scream. Magda, his wife, walked beside him. Alice expected a salute but Goebbels only kept his clenched fist against his mouth. The thunder of the American bombs and approaching Russian boots echoed in the space getting closer second to second.

Magda squeezed her husband's free hand tightly. "You are the chancellor now."

Gerda's face shook with sorrow about to erupt. She and Alice had been here in the bunker since January. No sunlight, no fresh air. They had only hope, and now that was gone. Gerda looked up at Goebbels, the new leader. She shook her head and ran out.

Alice didn't know any of the other assembled officers. They looked to Goebbels, each one of them, like a portrait of fear. They had been promised a place in an empire and now reality was setting in. One of the men put his hat under his arm.

"We must surrender," Goebbels' voice sounded shattered. He looked at his wife for a long moment before snapping his fingers and leaving the room. Alice and Magda were alone.

Alice felt fear and sorrow bubble to the surface. Magda pulled her into a hug. They had never been close. The pain and fear were enough to unite them at that moment. They cried together, the latest of the bombs to drop on Berlin shook the walls and dirt crumbled softly on their heads.

Magda held out her hand, revealing a tiny white pill.

"Cyanide, quick and painless."

Alice couldn't speak. Magda had no idea what she was suggesting, Alice had not told a soul. She just shook her head.

"The Russians are ruthless, there is not a woman they leave alone. They will beat you, rape you, beat you again. You are just another German bitch who must pay."

She put the pill in Alice's hand. "You bite it, break the shell, Alice you must take it."

Alice closed her hand over the pill. She wondered about this woman's six children whom she saw eating candy just hours ago. The future of Germany. "Joseph is writing the surrender, we are surrendering. Perhaps we will be fine."

Magda rubbed Alice's head putting some of her dark blonde hair behind her ear. "It doesn't matter my dear. It is too late for Germany."

"How did this happen?"

"The Fuhrer bit off more than he could chew..."

"No, he was a great leader, what the Allies did to us at Versailles..."

Magda nodded before she turned and walked away. "It is too late to argue, the war is lost."

Alice looked at the door and thought of the dead couple on the other side, married for just the last day of their lives. Her heart broke for them. For Germany. She looked at the pill and knew she had to talk to her Henry. She put the pill in her pocket.

Alice walked out into the greater bunker. The hall was crowded with SS officers who were running to meet with Goebbels. Like a miracle, he was in the group of sergeants who passed her. He made eye contact with her but she knew he wouldn't stop. She walked beside him picking up her pace to follow.

"Alice, I can't now," Heinrich Hitzinger whispered.

She grabbed him by the arm and pulled him away from the group. The reality was the world was ending, what did it matter if they were seen together now? She pulled him into a corner. His bold blue eyes that she had fallen in love with were dull with a pain they all felt. He was the only light for her in the bunker. They had met and flirted many times when he came to see the Fuhrer. She assumed he had a wife and children. The pain and fear of the bunker washed away any concern she had. When they were together, she escaped for those wonderful moments.

Now they lived with the absolute terror of knowing everything they loved was ending. That reality hung over him like an albatross. Away in the corner he leaned in and kissed her. Their lips met and for the briefest of moments, she felt bliss. It all melted away.

He pulled away from the kiss. "I'm sorry Alice, they are coming. The Russians…"

"I'm pregnant," Alice cut him off. "Two months now, I'm sorry it was never the right time to tell you, I kept waiting for the war to turn but…"

She knew he was struggling with how to react. It was the duty of men in the Reich to build a racially pure nation, Boorman had taken a second wife. She wanted him to respond with joy. Who could summon joy in this moment? A child is a beautiful thing but what Germany would be left? They were supposed to be married months ago but Heinrich worked closely with the SS commander Himmler, as his most trusted aid, they traveled often and Alice had to stay with the Fuhrer. He had always treated her with respect, it was easy to fall in love while losing a war but impossible to marry despite promises. Their love was mostly a secret.

"My child," he whispered.

Alice held out the pill. "Magda gave me this but I can't. Not now, she can't expect me…"

"You have no idea what she has done to protect her children."

"Is it true Himmler negotiated with the Swedes? They could help us."

Heinrich shook his head. "No deals, we are on our own."

"He betrayed the Fuhrer for nothing." Alice put her hand on her belly and looked up at him. "So, we die here tonight?"

Heinrich looked around the corner and held her hand. "Himmler can still save us. We knew this day would come."

"You have a plan."

"A secret, only a few officers know, we have only a few seats in the truck."

"You were coming for me?" Alice was close to rage.

"Of course," Heinrich rubbed her shoulders. "Go to your quarters and pack."

She turned to leave and Heinrich grabbed her arm. "We have to move quickly, once the surrender is accepted our orders will be meaningless. If the Russians capture us…"

"I know."

"We must leave the country; we will never be Germans again. Can you do that?"

Alice hadn't thought of that but the alternative was unthinkable. She nodded.   He smiled to try and reassure her before leaving, but how could she feel anything but fear?

# CHAPTER
# ONE

THE MEMORIES LIVED in the shadows and Noah Samvovich couldn't escape them. He slept with the light on. Still, the horrors lived like monsters in what darkness they could find. His memories became an eternal night. Twenty-six days ago, maybe twenty-seven at this point, he stopped looking at his watch at night because it reminded him that he had not slept. The only sound sleep he got was on the nights when the alcohol drowned the monsters. He had made it to central Germany that day traveling with the 89th infantry division, they marched alongside the 602nd tank division.

His skills with languages, Yiddish, Russian, French, and improving German got him out of the Army Rangers and into OSS, on paper he was headquartered in neutral Istanbul, but he traveled wherever the war needed him to be. Most of the missions were classified, dangerous and without uniforms. He fought with French Resistance cells during the worst days of the occupation and barely remembered the bitter cold of Minnesota where he sent vague letters home.

He was born in Minsk, but his earliest memories were of the synagogue on the south side of Minneapolis where his mother ran a daycare and his father ran a Torah study. He wasn't yet three when his parents left Russia a full year before the revolution and no matter how many times he asked, they wouldn't tell him about the journey. His mother only reminded him he should be thankful to be so young that he couldn't remember. His brother and sister were American-born, and they never asked. He was the only child in the house that understood the arguments they had in Russian.

They arrived on April 4th, 1945 just after dawn at the Ohrdruf camp, hours before the U.S. Generals and the media he had assembled. Eisenhower led cameramen and every soldier under his command to see for themselves the inhumanity. They had marched through the night and knew the Germans had retreated. It had been hours since any Germans had fired in their direction. They had relaxed, a certain safety and peace of mind came over the men marching toward the rising sun. They were happy to not face the German army but had no idea what they were about to witness.

Noah noticed the smell first. Foul is too weak a word for it. They smelled the camp long before it was even on the horizon. The dawn was bright enough to not spare them any sight. The infantry unit was first to step into the camp at Ohrdruf. The Germans had left long ago, so the prisoners with  enough strength  walked  out into the muck. Clothes dirty and smelling of the grave were piled near the gates and Noah thought they were covering skeletons. Some moved on the pile, just enough to show they were clinging to life. The bones were covered by skin that hardly resembled anything he had seen on humans before.

A skeleton stepped toward him, the skull had broken teeth and eyes that were barely lit by life. It took him entirely too long to realize that the person before him was a woman, just barely a woman by any measure of humanity. She fell at Noah's feet and grabbed his hand to kiss it. Not a minute has passed since that day he doesn't feel the bones of her hand against his own, or see the paper-thin skin of her face. It took strength she didn't have to weep, her body was weak yet produced tears, she tried to shout prayers in Yiddish but Noah barely heard her.

"Ir zent frey" He told her. You are free.

It was a lie. They were never free again, the night-mares were chains the Nazis left on their minds. Goddamn them, Noah thought to himself a thousand times every day. The camp at Ohrdruf was the first the Allies had freed, but the Russians had found more camps in Poland and the western front. 10,000 souls at Ohrdruf was a misery hard to understand, but small compared to the inhumanity at Auschwitz.

A month later her voice as faint as a gentle breeze still echoed in his ear. Noah wanted to sleep, he needed to be sharp if the word was given. He knew he had to sleep but he listened for the phone. The farmhouse was a resistance command center as much as a safe house. Each time he heard the ring he believed it was the time. The Russians were closing in on Berlin, the Americans were coming up from the south and he was here waiting for the orders. His mission was simple. Heinrich Himmler was the final solution. He more than any person after Hitler had designed the horrors. He was Noah's target. Noah would kill as many Nazis as he could but he would never sleep again if Hitler and Himmler lived.

The last phone call had been short. The American General Patrick was not known for conversation. *"Evening Sammy."* Noah hated the nickname the Generals had given him. *"They found another camp yesterday outside Munich at Dachau. Big one..."*

He may have said something else but Noah honestly didn't remember. He tried to sleep, fading in and out of restlessness until...

Ring.

Noah looked at his watch - 4:37 AM. The second ring echoed through the farmhouse. The sky outside his window was still dark. He jumped out of bed. He didn't want anyone else to answer. He was in the living room by the third ring.

He answered. The voice spoke Russian. Vlady was not his real name, but the Russians and British intelligence agencies had arranged for them to meet on a mission in Paris. They both should have died many times, and the respect between them was genuine.

"He's dead," Spoken in Russian.

"Who?" Noah responded in English.

"The great Fuhrer is no more," in broken English. "Goebbels is drafting a surrender."

"How did he die?"

"We don't know yet, it will take some time to find the body, the German public doesn't know yet."

"Will Stalin accept the surrender?"

"You don't have time to waste."

"Shit," Noah took a breath. "Thank you Vlady."

"Himmler will execute the Alpine Hawk you understand. In your Germany, in the south."

"Understood."

Noah hung up the phone. His French friends were gathered at their bedroom doors looking at him. "Go back to sleep," He shooed them off and was dressed and out the door before any of them went back to sleep.

# CHAPTER
# TWO

May 1st 1945 4:40 AM Berlin

ALICE HADN'T SLEPT through the night since they came
to the bunker, tonight it was impossible. Heinrich held her tight
and he seemed to know when fear pushed sleep away. He whispered to her telling her to sleep and she did for a few moments
at a time when she could. It didn't last long. She had grown
accustomed to the bombs falling, they had a pattern and you
could trick the mind to believe it was a late summer storm. She
closed her eyes and listened to the low rumble, and slowly
a picture of her bedroom window in Munich came to her. The
sound that kept her awake was not the rumble but the faint
echo of the single shot that killed the Fuhrer. It conspired to
keep her sleep short and restless. When the order was given to
leave it only took her five minutes to gather her belongings,
four outfits, and a picture of her family on vacation in the Alps
when she was a teenager. She wondered about her brothers
who served on the Western front. Months had passed since she
heard from them.

"Henry?"

His breath was soft and she didn't want to wake him. He
shifted.

"Henry, where do you think we will go?"

"Somewhere safe."

That seemed impossible, safety was just not possible. She understood it was beyond Germany, that she may have to hide her family photo. Take it out of the frame and hide it. They were leaving Germany and everything they had ever known. She just wanted to know. She didn't want to ask, but she had to know.

"Where? Please, sweetheart."

Heinrich took a deep breath; she nestled her head against his chest and listened faintly to his heart beating faster.

"Manchuria, Japanese-controlled China has more land than you can imagine. We can farm, we can relax…"

"What if the Americans beat them too?"

He never got a chance to answer as there was a knock at the door. Heinrich jumped up and answered the door. A young SS officer looked at Alice briefly and then back to Heinrich.

"The truck is waiting, time to go."

Heinrich turned back to her and signaled her to follow him. Alice grabbed her suitcase, she followed him to the door and the SS officer grabbed her arm. She looked into his cold blank eyes, it took a few seconds but she saw the fear he attempted not to show.

"I'm sorry Sergeant, but only direct family."

Alice looked at her love, she wanted to plead but his name wouldn't even come. She pictured Heinrich leaving without her, and the Russians entering the bunker-like rats and felt a little relief that she still had the little white pill. He wouldn't. He couldn't. Enough time passed for her heart to break, for rage to swirl like the first winds of a storm.

"We don't have time for this," said Heinrich.

"Gruppenfuehrer gave clear orders, only immediate family…"

"She is the mother of my child-to-be."

Alice didn't speak but felt relief that he was fighting for her. The anger faded.

The young officer looked at them both. Alice watched Heinrich slowly drop his right hand closer to his pistol and unhook his holster. The young officer loosened his grip on her arm. Alice wrenched it away.

"There are limited seats."

They could hear people running in the tunnel, it could be their seats. Heinrich barely contained his rage. "Think carefully young man."

The young officer nodded, "If anyone asks Wagner married you both before he married Eva and the Fuhrer."

Heinrich didn't care about the conversation, he grabbed Alice's hand and they ran. They turned into the main tunnel and there were several officers walking and running at a quick pace. They carried suitcases. A few were still in uniform, most were not. They walked for what seemed like miles in the limited light of the tunnel. Heinrich dropped his uniform shirt and SS hat along the way, just leaving them forever along the length of the tunnel.

No one spoke. The only sound, the shelling and gunfire were getting louder as the tunnel climbed closer to the surface. After a while, the sounds of battle faded. They must have passed under the Russian advance. The light was so dim that when they were still a ways from the entrance the light hurt Alice's eyes.

They came out into the sun and it had not lit the full sky, but it was as bright as noon in the desert to eyes that had been underground for four months. A truck designed for moving troops waited with the engine on. Heinrich helped to lift her onto the truck and for a moment she looked back at Berlin.

She hadn't meant to, but she had to look. She gasped. Berlin was a wasteland. Devastation stretched as far as she could see. Only broken shells that had once been homes or buildings remained. The city was erased. Like a chalk drawing washed off a blackboard, parts of the city didn't even have rubble, with only ash and craters remaining.

Heinrich pushed her into the truck. A man was helping his son to nestle into a tiny spot between his wife and another officer. There was nowhere left to sit. One of the SS men smiled and offered her a spot on the bench. She sat down just as the truck began to move. Heinrich shut the back gate and sat there with a rifle. Alice knew there was still reason for fear but the comfort of fresh air was enough for her to feel better. It took a few breaths before she tasted the ash in the air. She coughed out the ashes of Berlin, the ashes of Reich, and prayed for their escape.

# CHAPTER
# THREE

THE SUN ROSE over Nazi Germany for the last time. Noah was positive it was the end for them as he saw the dull glow poke through the clouds. They were only a short walk from the border, once the news reached the world that Hitler was dead everything would change. He couldn't be certain what borders would remain in a few days. He felt a little regret that he didn't kill the bastard himself but there was peace knowing that Hitler was gone.

The village was already awake, the farmers were up feeding their animals, and the sound of roosters greeting the dawn could trick you into forgetting the war was still raging. There were no friends of the Nazis in these hilltop villages, and Noah got nothing but respectful nods from husbands and wives as he passed. From the early days of the war, this was a resistance town. They had no idea how close to the end they were and he couldn't tell them. Not until his last mission was done.

The town was small, with only a few storefronts, a blacksmith, a shoemaker, a general store that sold farm supplies, the cafe, and the hotel. The hotel was mostly empty before the

Allies came into town. It was a regional base of operations and home to two British and U.S. Command staffs. The family that operated the hotel had been shot in the street by the SS for having a basement full of his Jewish employees and their families. The families had spent the better part of two years in the basement, and now that the Allies had taken the town, the same basement kept their prisoners.

Noah walked into the hotel and already, at this early hour, Private Cobb with the thick bottle glasses welcomed him. "Sergeant Samvovich, is General Patrick expecting you?"

"Doesn't matter lad," Field Marshal Brunner of the British Army was coming down the steps. "I was expecting him."

"Not that it matters Cobb, but the old man called me."

Private Cobb nodded. He didn't have the eyes for the front lines but ran operations close to it for more than a tour. He had the respect of everyone as he could've gone back to Jersey long ago. "Coffee sir?"

Noah smiled. "Wake the dead with it son."

Brunner waited until they were alone in the lobby. "Can you believe it?"

"We can't take the chance not to."

Brunner nodded. "Alpine Hawk?"

Noah nodded. "Do I have to ask?"

Brunner sighed. "Under the Americans' authority."

"General Patrick," he said the name like a swear. "He's a racist."

"Ohrdruf changed him."

Noah didn't believe it. Patrick was a southern boy, he refused to command a unit of Harlem Hellfighters in Italy. Patton wasn't much better but took the command for him. Patrick hated Germans but he was not a fan of Jews, he had never been shy about hinting this to Noah. The General was as mean as a drill sergeant before his first cup of coffee.

The General's office door opened. The tall imposing man waved them in. He was hardly in the shape he demanded of the men under his command. Brunner didn't wait to be invited and walked in before Noah. Cobb handed him his coffee just in time. Patrick went around the hotel manager's desk that he inherited. The hotel manager's family was still in a picture propped up on the desk. Patrick had added a picture of his family back in Georgia. Noah thought it was odd to keep a picture of the family that was murdered, but perhaps General Patrick wanted the reminder.

Patrick smiled. "The bastard is dead."

"The Russians have not confirmed it, but they have soldiers on the inside trying to negotiate surrender."

Patrick laughed. "How is that going?"

Brunner shook his head. "Not well, Stalin is not interested. The SS leadership will try to escape."

"Himmler," said Noah. "For months he has been planning a mission called Alpine Hawk, top SS leadership plan to escape to Manchuria."

"We're beating the Japs," Patrick offered them cigars. Brunner took one.

"Trials, endless trials." Noah's voice already dripping with rage. "They will blame Hitler, they were following orders. We can't let that happen."

"What are you saying, son?" Patrick took a puff.

"The surrender is coming, this is it," said Noah. "The last night to kill Nazis."

Patrick took a deep drag on the cigar, and laughed. "Don't get me wrong I like the sound of that. That is why I called you. The last thing this world needs is a bunch of Nazis lying through a thousand trials. What do you need?"

"I need him. Our friend in the basement."

"I had a feeling you'd say that. Some weapons are best left in the holster, if it weren't for orders our friend would be ashes to ashes already."

Noah leaned forward in his chair. "You need to trust me. I can handle him."

"I wasn't sure your kind believed in him."

"After seeing the camps no monster seems impossible."

"I suppose not," Patrick stood and looked out the window at the sky and the growing light of dawn.

Noah looked at Brunner and back to Patrick. "Now is the moment to let this dog off the chain."

The sun came through the window and shined across Patrick's face. "He'll be sleeping soon."

"He'll want to hear my offer," Noah waited.

General Patrick sat back at his desk and opened the drawer. He brought out a large wooden cross. He placed it on the desk and pushed it slowly closer to Noah.

"He don't fear your star I'm afraid."

# CHAPTER
# FOUR

<u>May 1<sup>st</sup> 1945 5:45 AM. Outside of Berlin</u>

ALICE TRIED to close her eyes, but the ride was as bumpy as it could be. The roads were bombed out and the truck didn't absorb any of it. Every hole, every bump and the flat board under her hit her tailbone. The mother next to her tried in vain to quiet her crying baby. The toddler was the only person who had a voice left. She carefully watched Heinrich at the back of the truck with his rifle ready.

From the open back of the truck they watched the Fatherland that was no more pass in their wake. Not even trees or grass remained. The sky was gloomy like a cloudy day but she knew it was smoke from endless fires blocking the sun. Alice looked down at a five-year-old boy nestled between his mother's legs. He held on to a Luftwaffe toy bomber. The boy caught Alice staring.

The boy whispered. "Don't worry lady, Commander Göring will save us."

Alice nodded and wished she had this child's faith. His mother had an SS pin on her collar, she was a mother but also an officer. She leaned over and her baby finally relaxed a bit. "We will make the new Fatherland, even better."

"I'm Alice, and you are?"

The young mother seemed to hesitate. "Irma. And my son is Josef."

The boy waved his toy plane to acknowledge his mother's introduction.

"You are with Heinrich my dear?" Irma smiled.

Alice nodded. "I'm a secretary, and was working with the Fuhrer."

Irma was surprised, it turned to sadness. She didn't have time to feel the sorrow. They went into darkness, they all gasped.

"Tunnel."

It was Heinrich's voice. The truck stopped under faint light. One small bulb lit the hastily constructed tunnel. The door of the truck opened and they heard boots stomping back. The SS officers still in uniform started to undress. Then a light appeared at the end of the tunnel. One bright light getting closer and the sound of a small engine. It was a motorcycle with a sidecar. Heinrich jumped out. The sidecar was loaded with clothes. Civilian clothes. The driver put on a Russian army trench coat.

The last thing out of the sidecar was a stack of blankets. Alice had to hold her nose when Heinrich dropped them in the truck. They were foul, instinctively she looked away but the smell was there.

"Jews smell of rats always," Irma said before cooing to her child to be quiet.

Alice looked back to see the Star of David etched on the blankets. It was a memory from years ago when the Jews were being loaded onto trains. Some of the children had these thin blankets. Her father applauded the trains. "Alice it is good for them, to be among their own kind. Good for Germany, good for them."

The motorcycle came back to life, it roared in the tunnel, like a bomber low in the sky. It passed and the  Russian truck  moved. Heinrich was just clipping his belt and jumping on board when they picked up speed. It was a disguise, all of it. They would hide like Jews, it made her sad and she had to just put her hand on her belly and think of her boy. She just knew it was a little boy.

# CHAPTER
# FIVE

PRIVATE COBB FUMBLED the keys and he had to pick them up. He searched through the two dozen keys to find the one that would unlock the basement. He was scared or delaying on purpose. Brunner clutched the cross so tight his knuckles were white. Noah could faintly hear the man saying a prayer. Rather than talk to god, Noah reached in his jacket and unlocked his holster. He knew logically that particular weapon was useless but it gave him comfort more than any prayer.

"Here we go, the right one." Cobb nervously smiled and turned the key. He stood back from the door. He had no intention of going in. The basement was dark except for two small windows near the ceiling that were letting in just enough light to see the cell bars. The Army Corps of Engineers had built it overnight to hold a dozen prisoners but only two remained.

A sweaty German slept on a cot pushed to the far side of the beam of light. Steel bars separated them but Noah didn't blame the German for still being afraid. The creature hid in the shadows. There was a pine box big enough to be a coffin in the cell. It was empty for the moment.

Brunner flipped on the light. Cockroaches and rats would

have scurried but they were lined up dead and drained of blood next to the coffin. The creature looked human, he stood now with dignity not fit for a monster in prison eating rats. He was shirtless, imposing, and tall. He didn't need to have muscles, the body the devil gave him had impossible strength.

"Reiter?"

"Count Reiter," the creature said.

"We don't recognize your title," Brunner squeezed the cross but held it at his side.

"Neither did the Nazis," the Count smiled.

Noah looked at the German in the next cell, he was sweating despite the cool temperature. He was a survivor. He knew exactly what Count Reiter was capable of.

"No, they didn't," Noah stepped closer to the bars.

"I was defending my home." Count Reiter was indeed the ancestorial owner of the castle that had been rotting for 120 years in the Carpathian Mountains. He was said to be born in a time before America existed. The exact year was unknown. The Nazis wanted to take it, clean it up and make it a resort, a getaway for the monsters who killed Jews and gypsies in the camps. Two hundred Nazis died in one night trying to take the castle.

"I respect what you did in Romania."

"I was content to sleep for ages."

Brunner was a leader of men, a veteran of battle and he stood before this thing disgusted and terrified. Noah could sense it coming off him, and he knew Reiter could, he probably sensed both of their increased heartbeats. This was how the creature hunted, it sensed blood at a distance the way tracking dogs smell. This was why it killed so many Nazis so effortless- ly. "I thought we were just food to you," said Brunner.

"I was once human."

"Centuries ago," Brunner retorted.

"I assure you I hate the Nazis too, I consume to survive the things they do, the way they wield misery is an insult to monstrosity."

Noah nodded. "We agree on that. There is nothing the Nazi deserves except oblivion."

Reiter walked as far into the cell as he could but Noah didn't back away. The small beam of light did more to stop him than the bars.

"They wanted my blood to steal my strength, Strigoi, the wolf-man, and banshees all. The Nazis came to steal us from the shadows. How are you any better?"

"I am here to give you a choice," said Noah.

He held up the chains that bound his wrists. They were old heavy chains, covered in flaky rust. Noah grinned. They both knew Reiter could snap those chains in an instant. Standing closer now Noah realized the bars of the cage that held him in were pure silver. Even those felt flimsy.

"I feel the change in the air." Reiter was as close as he could get. "Hitler is dead, isn't he?"

Brunner nodded. "Rats are scurrying to get off the ship."

"Why come to see me? What choice are you giving me?"

Noah looked at his watch, sick of the games. "We need you for a mission, it is dangerous but we want the same thing."

"Blood?" Reiter wanted a reaction.

"Yes, Nazi blood," Noah sounded excited. "Flowing like a river, we wait and they will live, they could escape and live free in hiding, worse they could stand trial, blame it all on Hitler and the orders he gave them and escape justice. Real justice."

Brunner had enough. "Bloody hell, will you help us?"

Reiter smiled and for the first time, Noah saw his fangs. "I'm in."

# CHAPTER
# SIX

May 1st 1945  6:05 AM. Liberated France near the German
border

MARION SMELLED the eggs frying in her room. She wanted to get out of bed and the idea of coffee pulled at her, but the idea of sleeping in wasn't bad either. She nestled into the thick blanket, ready to sleep another hour when she heard the sound of a motorcycle coming up the country road. She was pretty sure she knew who it was but grabbed her pistol. She kept the ruby loaded, it could be anyone coming down the road, she used its barrel to push open the curtains and watched the road.

The boys downstairs were scrambling to load their rifles. They'd been waiting for bad news. The motorbike came into view and she relaxed. It wasn't a Nazi, the opposite. Noah Samvovich had arranged for this house, he had wanted to keep her close, he never said why, but they knew it was his special prisoner. Marion wanted the creature dead, but Noah saw him as a weapon. His hatred ran deeper with each passing day. The war consumed everyone in Europe but Noah had a weight on his shoulders no one envied.

Marion grabbed a holster for the Ruby and a hat to cover her bed hair. By the time she came downstairs, Herzog and Mallory were putting away their weapons.

"It's Noah," Mallory picked up his coffee and followed her out onto the porch. Greg Mallory was a British SAS officer who had survived enough suicide missions to decide he was finishing the war on his own terms. Kurt Herzog turned off the gas on the stove and was not in a rush to see Noah. He was a German dissident, who eventually played Nazi to infiltrate the government. When he was found out he escaped with Mallory. That made him useful but Noah and Herzog never trusted each other fully.

Marion was new to Europe and the war theater. She put on the act as best she could. No fear on the surface, no weakness or they would send her home. For now, she was safe. Romania had bonded the three of them. She showed up just before the mission to capture Reiter. The creature had been her father's obsession. She never thought he was real, but since her father's death and against her wishes, she knew more about the creature than anyone.

Marion stepped out into the unseasonably chilly morning as Noah took off his helmet. He was a tall and handsome Jewish man. It was dangerous having his face in Europe. He was clearly Jewish, no star needed, and Marion respected him for that. Mallory and Herzog assumed that she fancied him, but men didn't understand that women respected men they had no desire to sleep with. She had found that, in the face of death almost daily during war, the men would bed nearly anyone.

"I hope you have good news." She tried to sound neutral.

"The best, Hitler ate a bullet last night."

Mallory laughed in disbelief and looked at Marion. "My French is not great but I heard nothing on the radio."

"Russians have not found the body yet."

"Nazis surrender yet?" Herzog stepped behind her.

"Germany?" Noah shook his head. Herzog tried to separate the Germans from the Nazis. After walking through the camps, Noah was no longer debating the issue. "They will soon, but that is why I am here."

"The clock is ticking then," added Mallory. "I take it Himmler and the SS are trying to escape."

"Bastards," Herzog said under his breath, too angry to even raise his voice.

Marion knew where this was heading. He wanted to take Reiter and unleash him on the Nazi bastards. The Nazis had killed her mother in Pittsburgh and kidnapped her father Professor George Riverwood. All in a vain attempt to capture or stop Reiter. Marion swore revenge and went to the CIA herself to convince them that she understood her father's work and could help them beat the Germans.

It was an adventure for a woman who was 23 years old and accepted to her choice of graduate schools when the war ended. School could wait, first, she had to put a stake in the heart of the monster that had feasted on her father.

"He'll kill the Nazis but at what cost Noah?"

"I'm taking you, and when the mission is done..." He made a fist over his heart.

Mallory wasn't hiding his feelings. His expression said it all. "It is a big risk, you sure there is no other way?"

"There are other ways sure..." Noah decided not to finish that.

"You want to hurt them," Marion sighed. "I get it Noah, but it is a huge risk."

Noah stood there silent and determined. It had been weeks, maybe longer, since she'd seen him and there was a pain in his eyes. He was an angry man before but it was deeper now. She understood, she heard the rumors of what the Nazis had done. He wasn't thinking clearly.

"Just let me in there Noah, I'll end it right there, if we take him back into the world my god think of the consequences."

"Briefing is in one hour, we don't have a second to debate, Himmler and his SS will escape tonight, you hear me? Tonight, I will not allow it. I will not watch them wave white flags, or throw themselves at the mercy of a court. Come on Mallory, you know what they would do."

"We could sit here and let the war end."

Noah put on his helmet and walked to his bike. "You could?"

Mallory just stared at his old friend for a long moment. "No, I can't."

Marion had heard enough. She knew they were going. She thought it was a terrible idea but she swore she would not let that creature escape. "We'll be there at seven, come on boys we need our breakfast."

# CHAPTER
# SEVEN

NOAH CARRIED the chalkboard into the basement and set it down in front of the cell. He spun it to the side that was empty before Brunner flipped on the light. The Nazi in the other cell had disappeared as he'd asked for. Reiter was fully dressed now, and wearing a button-up shirt, his hair was wet and combed back.

General Patrick and Field Marshal Brunner pulled up chairs. Noah left the door open. He knew Riverwood would never leave Reiter alive, she didn't care about the war, only her father's mission. Destroy the creature.

Mallory and Herzog couldn't resist. They would be here.

Reiter stood up and the chains tightened with a creak and pop as he inched closer. His veins were obvious under his pale skin. Noah understood Reiter was not human anymore, it was impossible not to wonder how his body worked. There was biology involved but also the darkest of magic.

"Well, this mission is important now isn't it?" Reiter mock saluted. "I know these old men are not going so tell me, so will it be it just one Jew and myself to stomp out the dying embers of the Third Reich?"

"Don't be so modest Count," Brunner got comfortable in his seat. "We know how many you have killed."

Reiter grinned. "The world is at war and you two didn't get so powerful for your kind nature. No, we all have blood on our hands, the question is what shade of red?"

Patrick tilted his head a bit. "Does he think he is Goddamn Shakespeare?"

"He does have a certain flair," said Brunner.

"I was born in a more elegant era."

"Are you shitting me," Patrick grinned. "Tell me Count you ever heard of a shower? We have those."

Reiter stared at General Patrick. "Our friends are here." The Field Marshal got up to welcome the newcomers to the meeting. Noah relaxed a little but he never doubted.

Noah wrote in chalk Alpine Hawk as Marion, Herzog, and Mallory came into the room.

Reiter smiled. "Ah yes, old friends, what a reunion this is."

"Shut up," Marion said as she leaned against the wall. Noah didn't blame her for being uneasy in the presence of the creature.

"Miss Riverwood, I feel an obligation to tell you that I did not want to kill your father…"

"We are here to explain the mission." Brunner stood up beside Noah at the chalkboard.

"…He would have killed me if not for curiosity, he was so close to the monster he studied his whole life, he could not help himself but…"

"Shut your mouth!" Marion lifted the wooden stake and pointed it at Reiter. She had it in a loop on a belt, her father's belt. He was made for this, they needed him for this kind of hunt. Both Mallory and Noah got in her way. Noah was surprised by her strength as she pushed him back. He had to set his feet to hold her back. Reiter laughed. Noah looked straight into her hazel eyes. She looked young, her skin was lightly freckled but Noah knew her to be fierce and intelligent.

"Marion, the mission." Noah looked at her and wanted her to understand. "I want you there."

Reiter sat back down in the corner of his cell. "The expert's daughter, keep her on a leash Jew or I might as well die in this cage."

Noah pointed at an empty chair. She had no reason to take orders from him, she was in no position of service and this mission was not sanctioned. He just hoped at that moment she respected him enough to sit down. They communicated many things silently. She hated this. All of it. Marion spun the stake and slipped it back into the loop on her belt. Mallory sat down first, and Herzog remained standing, his arms behind his back. He was the most skeptical. That was fine, he was a former SS and Noah didn't trust him as much as Mallory did.

Brunner tapped the blackboard with a pointer to get their attention. "This is not just another Tuesday. The Battle of Berlin is ending on a commie holiday. As we speak General Hans Krebs is trying to hammer out a ceasefire with Vasily Chuikov of the Soviet 8th Guards Army. After the Nazi minister of propaganda Joseph Goebbels wrote a letter surrendering, he killed himself with his wife in the park. The terms could be accepted in a matter of hours, or it could take days. When that happens, our ability to get swift justice will be lost. The clock on this war is ticking faster now. Before time runs out we have one last mission that must be completed."

Brunner nodded to Noah. "Alpine Hawk is the code name for a mission planned by Heinrich Himmler."

"Weasel," Herzog said under his breath, but everyone heard it.

"Watch what you say about weasels," Mallory tapped his knee.

"No one short of Hitler is more responsible for the crimes of the Final Solution than Himmler," Noah added.

Brunner nodded. "In his role as commander of the SS, he remains one of the most powerful figures in Germany. However, according to multiple sources, Himmler has tried to negotiate deals and surrender with multiple governments over the last few weeks."

"I reckon they told him to sod off properly," Mallory laughed.

"Indeed," Noah spun the chalkboard around. He pointed to an elaborate drawing of a mountain and the Nazi compound.

They had been working on it for days, and the details matched grainy photos taped to the board.

"Hitler was stubborn and determined to die if the Reich failed. Himmler on the hand, the poor lad has only escaped now, and he has been promised a home in Manchuria. He has convinced one hundred and fifty SS officers and a few of their spouses to join him." Brunner pointed to the drawing of the mountain. "The Nazis have built several cottages and mansions throughout the Alps as southern command centers. This fortress is Himmler's last stand."

Noah drew the last detail and turned around. "The Nazis cut the top off this peak and put in a three-hundred-and-twenty-foot landing strip. It has a mansion with enough rooms and beds for a hundred Nazis. This is Himmler's fallback; he is flying all one hundred and fifty Nazis off this mountain."

"Let me guess, they will be bombing the only bridge in and out of the mining the roads," said Mallory.

"No turning back. Noah nodded. "They are using BV 114 cargo planes."

"Big suckers," General Patrick didn't know any more details than the rest of them.

"They still only carry 25 people," Herzog added.

"How many Nazis?" Reiter quipped.

Mallory laughed. Herzog gave his long-time partner a dirty look. Mallory just shrugged.

"Not every German is a believer." Said Herzog. "Most Germans thought he was a moron at first."

Noah stepped closer to Herzog. "These are believers. They had no mercy in their hearts for the human beings wasting away under their noses. Never forget that."

The General stood up to get a closer look at the drawing, he pointed at the board with his cigar. "An airstrip that short and in that space, they are only going to be able to land one plane at a time, and use a strong pull cable to slow down the landing planes like an aircraft carrier."

"The planes will begin landing tonight," Noah stopped. "Tomorrow technically at oh one hundred hours on May 2 and they will keep coming until they are all in the air heading to occupied Manchuria. If we fail, they live. We can't allow that."

Brunner collapsed his pointer. "They want to be in the air before daylight as they will be flying east into the sun."

Marion rolled her eyes. "Why not bomb the place to dust?"

Noah knew the answer, it was classified. The Nazis were developing the V-2 rocket and atomic weapons at the mansion. An OSS mission infiltrating the German science core had discovered the site. They already managed to poison two of the scientists. The Germans' research and advances were not to be lost. Noah was not sure what could be said and what had to remain secret. His pause must have been enough.

"Classified, right." Marion made no attempt to hide her anger. "We risk our lives for something you don't trust us to know."

"We still have a war to win with the Japs," The American General seemed annoyed to be explaining himself. The General pointed at Noah. "Our friend here knows more than I do. I understand your anger but focus on killin' them Nazis please."

"There is more. The top Nazis in Berlin are destroying evidence of their crimes, the last flight out will destroy the Eagle's Nest as well. That house can't be destroyed. No bombers will touch it." Noah gave a tap to his watch. "Nazis will be arriving all day, today. This is already happening," Noah writes NOW on the board. "We need to be in position when the sun goes down."

They all turn to Reiter.

"Very well, leave the rest to me."

# CHAPTER
# EIGHT

<u>May 1st 1945 7:28 AM. Liberated France near the German border.</u>

NOAH FOLLOWED General Patrick out of the basement. He exited like he was late for an important meeting. He felt the clock ticking, things were happening quickly.

"General, might I have a minute?"

Noah had resigned his commission and he didn't take orders from the General, but they both knew Noah was working for OSS. Early in the war, the agency was made up of rich privileged children of socialites and political figures. It was more like an Ivy League social club, and the General held it against him. Noah had worked out of Istanbul for most of the war, having the trust of the president and Langley to the point that he knew things this man with stars on his uniform did not. It bothered the General who never had a problem showing how racist he was. He didn't like taking orders from a man with no rank, a ghost budget, and the fact that Noah was Jewish didn't help either.

The General stopped as Brunner and Mallory continued to draw on the map behind them. Mallory, who was a veteran of several dangerous missions around Europe and behind enemy lines, may not have turned around, but Noah felt him paying attention to them He kept his voice quiet.

"You have a problem with the plan?"

The General laughed. "Oh Sammy, come on. You're asking me to hand you a grenade with the pin pulled. Not one day has passed since you and Riverwood brought that thing here I haven't thought about dragging it out into the sun."

"I'm glad you didn't."

"MacArthur gave me direct orders. So I kept your prisoner. It plays with your mind, you know that. Pops up in your dreams."

"We brought him in. I know what he is capable of."

"I hope that means you have a plan. For him, it."

"When the last Nazi is dead."

"We ain't gonna get them all Sammy," Patrick laughed.

Noah didn't, Patrick was making him uncomfortable in this moment. He was already celebrating.

Patrick looked away for a moment. "We won, it is over. Don't fight this war the rest of your life."

Noah didn't think Patrick could fully understand. These were Noah's people, when he closed his eyes, the nightmares waited. The mass graves, the skeletal bodies, the abandoned children, and that smell. There was nothing like the smell of the camps. It was impossible to walk inside those fences and imagine a human being could do that, not just to another human being, but to an entire nation  of them. Noah didn't want have this argument. General Patrick,  was a racist at heart and Noah had never trusted him. He might be able to go home and forget the war with his soul intact, and that was what Noah couldn't understand.

General Patrick nodded. "OK, son. One hundred and fifty of the worst Krauts seem worth the risk but damn it Sammy if that thing escapes."

Noah shook his head. "Destroying monsters is the mission General, why not let them do it to each other."

# CHAPTER
# NINE

ALICE WAS JOLTED awake by the bouncing of the truck. She was more shocked that she had managed to doze off. The filthy smell of the blanket with the Jewish star was something she had grown used to in the last few minutes. The idea that they would pass as Jews was just folly. They were healthy Germans after all, even in the stress of war they stayed strong. They could not pass for vermin, no one would believe it. Her thoughts went in all directions. One minute she was angry at what had become of them, what the Allies were doing to Germany—again. Then she would feel angry at what they had done to themselves.

She looked around at the dazed faces, she understood their disbelief. She too had believed that the Fuhrer would find a way to win the war. The driver had pushed the truck as fast as it would go. They had finally driven past the destruction and gotten into the countryside. Alice felt a certain relief seeing grass and little bits of sunlight breaking through the smoke-filled sky.

The smell of burning Germany was everywhere, there was no escaping that reality.

Heinrich finally relaxed a little, leaning back but still holding his rifle. He didn't seem as on guard as he had when they were still in Berlin. She wanted to believe he was only concerned about their child. He was a true believer. Even now.

No one spoke as time went on. The children cried a little, Alice understood. She had a good life early in the war. The Fuhrer was good to her, brought her to his retreats to Ober-salzberg, and she and Eva shopped together. She could have been jealous of the secretaries, but as the Fuhrer's companion, she treated them like sisters. Alice walked Blondie and spent quiet moments with the leader.

She held his hand once. She came into his office and found Adolf Hitler the man trying to stretch out the pain in his back. He was embarrassed and straightened up so quickly that he yelped out in pain. She ran to his side.

*"My Fuhrer please let me help."* He shook his head and tried unsuccessfully to stand straight. He gripped her hand through the pain as he moved to his desk. His skin was soft, his grip almost crushed her hand. He grinned. *"I am just a man you know."* He held his finger up as if to signal their secret. It was their secret but that tight grip and his pain never left her memory. The weight of the Fatherland on his shoulders, the man who had the strength to pull Germany from the ashes and confront the world for what it had done to them.

When she read the headlines from foreign papers that painted him a devil, or when he stood before the people and reminded them of their destiny. In moments of doubt or strength, she never doubted, not once, that the Fuhrer would remake the world to protect Germany.

The truck slowed. All the faces looked around nervously. Alice watched Heinrich come to attention and point his rifle. The love of her short life, the father of her child. She couldn't handle watching him die. The mother beside her hugged her youngest child. The truck stopped.

Silence, the sounds of birds chirping, the calm countryside. Who had stopped them? Was this the end? The mother shushed her child. They heard a voice.

"Thank goodness you made it!" Fluent German, they all relaxed.

Alice wanted to cheer. Heinrich jumped out of the truck and slung his rifle. He saluted, his arm outstretched. She had to lean in a bit to see whom he had saluted. The face was unmistakable. Himmler. Still, in his uniform, the man put up his hand to acknowledge the salute. The two men spoke.

Alice didn't trust Himmler. The Fuhrer didn't. Eva had told her that Himmler was trying to make deals with other countries. Her heart skipped a beat. *What if they were a part of one of his deals? What if these trucks were driving right into the hands of the Brits, the French, or the Americans?* She didn't think a deal could be made with the Russians, but Himmler was slick.

Heinrich smiled at his old commander, they shared more than a first name. Her Henry had worked closely with him in the Upper Rhine command center. She relaxed when Henry climbed back into the truck. He smiled in an attempt to reassure the proud Germans in the back of the truck. "We have met the caravan, we are heading south to the Alps, we have a few hours ride but as soon as we have our meals we must drive on. It is a bumpy road ahead, and not an ideal lunch but this day is another sacrifice for the Fatherland."

Heinrich turned away. Officer Einhard Goring shifted nervously across from Alice. All the weary faces turned to look at him. She could tell that Heinrich felt their fear and confusion, he smiled, a naked attempt to reassure them. Goring grunted, his displeasure made everyone in the truck uncomfortable.

Heinrich walked slowly and stood over him. "You have something to say?"

"Yeah," Goring threw the blanket to the floor of the truck. "Where is the Fuhrer now? Huh? While we hide like Jewish rats. Where is he?"

Alice almost screamed when Heinrich grabbed him. She knew in her heart that Heinrich was a soldier, but he had only been tender with her. Did Goring not even know that the Fuhrer was dead? Heinrich grabbed Goring with the hand that had just hours ago rested on her stomach feeling for the movement of their child.

"Do you want to die here, Goring? Wait for the Russians and tell them your problems with the Fuhrer?"

Goring grabbed the outside of the truck, to try desperately

to keep from being thrown out.   The man screamed "Heil Hitler! Please no."

Heinrich leaned closer, he whispered but the truck was so quiet they all heard it. "The seats are limited Goring; the new Fatherland has no place for doubt." Heinrich dropped him on the floor with a thud, his breath was labored and deep. He spun slowly to look at the faces.

"This is it. You want to run and beg the Soviets for mercy?"

Silence, except swaying trees in the light wind.   In another moment, it would've been beautiful. Alice closed her eyes and wished the war had never begun. The truck rumbled to life, and an SS officer came around to drop off a duffel bag with their meals. Heinrich took the bag of food. "Thank you."

Goring softly begged, some pretended not to hear him, Alice felt pity. The officer who delivered the food watched Goring cry for a moment. Heinrich shook his head, and the SS officer left and hit the truck twice. The truck pulled away now Alice watched as they passed a few more trucks parked on the road. One by one the trucks rumbled to life and came in behind them. A Mercedes that, a few days ago, had Nazi party flags and was outfitted with a large machine gun and a gunner pulled up behind the trucks. They were a caravan.

Goring dusted himself off but now his seat was gone. He had to sit on the floor. Heinrich grabbed the Jewish blankets and threw them off one at a time onto the side of the road. They didn't need to hide anymore. He kissed Alice on the forehead as he grabbed the last filthy blanket from her. He pulled out his lighter, all the eyes in the trucks watched as he lit the Jewish star on fire. A cheer broke out in the trucks he tossed it out on the road.

"We will never let the sacrifice of the Fuhrer and all we lost in this war be forgotten. We in this caravan are the future of the Reich." Heinrich looked right at Alice. Pride swelled inside her. He stepped closer and took her hand and he spoke only to her. "You carry the future, my love."

# CHAPTER
# TEN

GREG MALLORY HELD the nails and the hammer; he just needed the Count to get in the coffin. The rest of the team had their hands close to their weapons. Herzog wore a flamethrower with fuel strapped to his back. It was overkill but they knew all too well the danger. Reiter enjoyed the fear in the room far too much.

"Get in the bloody box already," Mallory pointed to it with the hammer.

He thought he was too old to fight in another great war. The Royal Navy had other ideas. When the blitz was over in late 1940, his orders came in a letter to the address that was already rubble. No one in Britain was immune to the war. For 52 days and nights, their building still stood. Five nights before the Blitz ended, his family rushed to the shelter, he built just days earlier. They barely had any room. Every earth-shattering rumble was terrifying. He had to trust his construction.

Allison and the boys kept up a brave face, right up to the moment when the lights flickered and went out on the 52<sup>nd</sup> night of the Blitz. His boys were ten and twelve years old. Allison held the youngest Thomas, and Greg held Christopher.

When the thunder rolled above them. Closer than ever. This time they heard the sound of the building coming down.

They had no light. Allison begged Greg to keep talking, so he did. It took 13 hours before they were pulled from the rubble. He made many promises to the boys under the rubble. The most important promise was that the war would end before they were old enough to fight in it. That he would make sure of it if he had to return to the service. Keeping production and economy going had become a duty. Allison had done her duty by taking a manufacturing job, and she was making bullets still as far as he knew.

He saw her once in '43 after a mission in Spain, OSS and MI-6 had arranged for them to spend a weekend together. Allison said little. She didn't want to know what he had done or what he would have to do still. They made love and she told him he could stay gone as long as he needed to, as long as he kept his promise to the boys. Now he had just one more night to keep that promise.

Reiter paused over the coffin. "She wants to kill me," He pointed at Marion.

"We all want to kill you," Herzog added.

Marion nodded but Noah shook his head. "I don't. We have a mission to complete."

Reiter grinned "The fuse is burning ever faster my dear. Remember that before you consider your actions."

"We're nailing it shut, no one can get you before you wake," said Mallory.

"He'll be dead to the world," Marion smiled. "Don't rest too easy count."

"Don't listen to her," Noah gave Marion an angry look.

Reiter walked closer to the coffin. He stepped inside and lowered himself. He crossed his arms to protect his heart and closed his eyes. Noah unlocked the cell, Herzog stepped forward and pointed the flame-thrower. The cell door swung open and Mallory and Noah put the top across. For just a moment Mallory looked down at Reiter. With his eyes closed, it was as if he had immediately reverted to being dead. His skin was more pallid, the color of shark skin. The cover fit tightly on top, and Mallory handed two nails to Noah.

Noah was acting calm, but this close up, Mallory saw the sweat on his forehead. Little fazed this spy, he needed this monster for the mission but he was just as afraid of it as they were. Noah waited as Mallory drove in the nails.

Noah looked back at Herzog and his Flame-thrower. "Relax." Herzog snapped off the gas and the weapon cooled.

Marion stepped up with a stencil and painted the side. The stencil added two Eagle's crests with swastikas and In German, it read. *"In memory of our fallen who died for the Fatherland."*

Mallory and Noah moved the heavy coffin onto two ropes, and they lifted them up until the make-shift handles were secured. Marion opened the back door and the sunlight shocked everyone. A beam of light shined across the casket. For a long moment, they waited to see if the wood had tiny holes or anything that might destroy their weapon.

Noah nodded and the four of them carried the coffin like pallbearers out into the morning. An Opel 3 truck that had survived a few years of the war was parked behind the hotel. If you looked closely, you might notice that the fabric on the cover was a British make and that the sides of the truck had hastily patched bullet holes.

It took all their strength to lift the coffin up into the truck. Field Marshal Brunner walked up to Noah and handed him the keys.

"You driving?"

"I was planning on it," Noah turned back and looked at the team. Mallory knew what Noah was thinking. He didn't want to leave them alone with the weapon. He was afraid they would let Marion end it. He was wrong of course, no one wanted to see Reiter let loose. Mallory put his hand up and caught the keys when Noah tossed them.

"You don't have to worry Noah, I am committed as you are, but" Mallory passed the keys to Herzog. "Let the German drive, who better to talk at checkpoints?"

Brunner handed the map to Herzog. "You ever been to Berchtesgaden?"

Herzog shook his head. "No, but I know where it is, south of Munich."

Noah hugged Brunner. "Hurry on lad, you have seven hours on German roads ahead of you."

Mallory saw the affection between the two men. Noah tapped his heart. "Tomorrow we celebrate."

Brunner looked at Mallory. It was uncomfortable between them. Brunner had a habit of sending him on suicide missions. Noah didn't seem to have a problem with this man who was content to send others to end the war. Men who gave those kinds of orders safely from behind the front bothered Mallory.

"Gregory, for the last time I promise to help your boys if…"

Mallory waved him off and climbed into the back of the truck. Noah climbed in last as the truck roared to life. *Was the war really ending?* He couldn't imagine Europe at peace. It seemed impossible.

Mallory lay down on the floor and turned his coat into a pillow. Rest while you can, he told himself. This may be the last night of the war but it was going to be a long one.

# CHAPTER
# ELEVEN

NOAH WISHED he could be as relaxed as Mallory and actually sleep. The Brit managed to even snore a few times. It was impossible for Noah; he had planned this mission weeks ago but had to wait until the conditions were right. It was Himmler's move first, and the intel was clear, the death of Hitler was the catalyst. That would start the chess pieces moving, the last days of the war. Everyone who'd fought had varying degrees of disbelief that this day would even come. The war had only lasted five years, but it had reshaped nations, destroyed cultures and threatened the entire world. Only five years but it felt like the world would end before the war itself.

As the truck bounced along, they were all quiet. The clock in his head told him they were getting closer to the border.

"I wonder if the checkpoints will still be there?" Marion asked.

"They will, the word has not spread this far. They are still fighting the war." Noah looked through a tiny window in the cab and saw only an empty road leading into the mountains. The truck slowed as they went uphill. Noah sat back on the bench and looked at Marion. She had a calm demeanor he didn't expect. They couldn't talk when the truck engine roared on the hill. She looked at Mallory's sleeping form, nothing woke him. She looked back at Noah as the truck coasted downhill. Now they could speak.

"This was what this whole thing was about?"

"What whole thing?"

Marion was easily annoyed. "Reiter, you wanted him for this all along."

Noah shook his head. "The Nazis took your father; they wanted Reiter, others like him. It was an arms race."

"And you thought to yourself, you know what, this young lady needs, a wartime experience."

"I'm sorry," Noah really was deeply sorry. "You were the only person who knew your father's work."

"I lied," Marion shrugged. "I never paid any attention to him when he talked about Strigoi, vampires, werewolves, or any of it. I thought he was crazy. My mother was happier when he was over here."

Noah grinned. "You fooled me."

"I just read his papers on the plane. I didn't think it was real."

Noah shook his head. "Why did you come?"

"I hoped he was alive; in the end, the crazy guy who wished he was Van Helsing is the only father I've ever had."

Mallory rolled over and sat up, betraying that he was listening. "I think you like being here. She is a thrill seeker, Noah."

"There may be truth to that," Marion let that hang in the air.

"We are going into the real war now sweetheart," Mallory wasn't being condescending even if it sounded like it. He really cared about her. She'd faced Reiter but the tough dame act was just that.

Noah kept his eyes on her. "If you thought your father was crazy, why avenge him?"

She gave Noah a harsh look, he felt her anger. She didn't have to tell him, but it was a stupid question. Herzog whistled in the front cab. Noah looked out the tiny window. The checkpoint was getting closer he could see the black uniforms in the distance. He snapped his fingers. "Nazis!" he said softly as they all readied their weapons.

Herzog slowed the truck as they pulled up to the border. It consisted of a retractable fence covered in razor wire and a tiny checkpoint house just big enough for the two guards.

"Run them down," Noah suggested.

"They will have a radio in the shelter. We leave them alive, they will put out a search for us." Herzog slowed the truck. "Leave them dead, someone might come to look for them."

They stopped fully, but Herzog kept the truck running. Their best bet was to fool them.

"What is this?" the guard yelled in German. "The border is closed."

Herzog put the truck in park and stepped out. "We are bringing home a hero of the Fatherland for burial in Munich."

The other guard walked toward the back of the truck. Noah signaled and they hid their weapons. Noah's pistol was under a blanket, and Mallory had his rifle under the bench.

"I brought French farmers to carry the casket," Herzog sounded relaxed and confident. "I will bring them back before nightfall."

Noah wasn't sure of every word Herzog said in German but he was following the story. The guard stared at them in the back of the truck. It had been weeks since he was behind the enemy lines and he felt fresh burning rage seeing those uniforms again. He had nerves, it rattled him just seeing them in the flesh. It brought back all the memories.

The Nazi spoke in rough French. "Is one of your French farmers a Jew?"

They all looked at each other. Noah was calculating how long it would take him to grab his pistol when Mallory responded in French.

"He is Algerian, a common mistake."

The Nazi relaxed only a little, his rifle dropped just a few inches. "He should not carry a hero of the Fatherland."

"He is only digging I assure you," Herzog added in German.

Noah made eye contact with the Nazi. He was young, skinny. Not an ideal choice to serve, but food was scarce at this point in the war. Noah felt the judgment, like arrows. He would have to shoot him, this deception was not working. If he went for his gun, the Nazi would shred them he was not...

BANG!

Marion held her pistol straight and the Nazi collapsed on the pavement with a chunk of his head in the grass. Noah lifted his pistol and jumped out. Herzog picked himself up and took the dead guard's rifle. The other guard ran towards the nearby tree line while fighting to unhook his sidearm holster.

Noah waved Mallory back and ran after the Nazi. His heart raced, as he closed the distance to the border guard. The young German tripped and struggled to get up. He wildly fired his pistol back. Noah didn't slow or even duck, he was never worried he would be hit. The Nazi made it into the trees. Noah could hear his breath in the woods it was so quiet.

Nazi hunting. The butterflies were gone, he had to focus on this moment given to him by God. He prayed each day for God to give him strength, and now he felt as if his prayers had been answered. He heard the bastard's heart beating like a drum, smelled his breath as if it was under his nose, and smelled his fear oozing from every pore.

The Nazi had climbed behind a rock. Noah might have had trouble finding him if he was not hyperventilating. This guard has never seen action before spending the last couple of months of the war at a random French border crossing. The Nazis had surrendered in every direction around him and this idiot still guarded his strip of road.

Noah followed the sound of his breath. He came around the rock and the Nazi shot past him. The gunfire echoed in the woods. Noah kicked his pistol out of his hand. He was a boy. If he was eighteen, he had not been for long. Noah felt a little sorrow creep in. This boy was still in school when the war began.

"Jew, goddamn Jew!"

Noah stared at the symbols all over the boy's uniform. Eagles and swastikas. His anger rivaled his fear. He wasn't good at cursing in English. The boy was confused to be here in the woods under the pistol of a Jew. He saw the boy's disbelief. It was the last day of the war. There was one thing he had to know.

Noah leaned in close enough to smell his breath. "Did you know what they did to my people?"

"You stink Jew!" The defiance was his answer.

"He is dead you know, Hitler. Your great Fuhrer ate poison and just to be sure..." Noah tapped his pistol against his temple. "Pop."

Tears. The young man was forming tears. "I will be honored to die for the Reich."

Noah nodded. "You will die, but there is no honor."

Tears welled up in his eyes, betraying the fear behind his defiance, "Dirty Jew."

"Tell the Fuhrer, I'm sending you all to hell."

# CHAPTER
# TWELVE

MARION JUMPED at the loud pop in the woods. It shook her bones and echoed like thunder. Mallory dragged the dead Nazi's body. He stopped at the sound. Herzog came out of the guard house with folded uniforms. They looked at each other. Her heart beat a little faster. *What if Noah was dead? He understood the mission better than anyone.* They would have to track down the Nazi that shot him and kill the bastard.

A second more muted BANG. Mallory's shoulder relaxed and he went back to pulling the body by its legs.

"Relax," Mallory told her. "The first shot was a Luger, the second was a Baretta. Noah got him."

Marion couldn't believe he could tell the difference, but he was pretty sure of himself.

The Nazi left a trail of blood and brains along the road. Herzog secured the extra uniforms in the truck and filled a bucket with water. They looked unfazed disposing of the body and blood. She understood they had done this type of thing many times. It wasn't until this moment that the gravity hit her —she'd killed the guard.

Mallory saw the look on her face and looked back to Herzog. He splashed the pavement with water and scrubbed the blood away. Marion stared at the blood as Mallory made it disappear.

"I didn't think you were the sentimental type, Marion?" Herzog already filled his next bucket.

"Your first time killing a man?" asked Mallory.

She thought about how young he had been. "He's barely a man."

Mallory nodded. "That's true, but forget his age."

He pulled the body out of sight around the building. Marion stared at the open door to the guard house and walked inside. Two desks were set up by the front window and there was just enough room for a sink, stove and two beds. Marion walked to the first desk. There was a picture of a German family, two elderly grandparents sat in the middle. Dressed in their finest, staged to show three generations. In flat black and white and a few years younger, she saw the face of the man she just shot.

Mallory grabbed the picture from her hand and crumpled it into a ball.

"Hey, what are you doing?"

He threw it in the trash. "No good will come from that Lassie," Mallory squared his shoulders. "You choose to stay on this mission, let's get something straight, this nation traded its humanity for something I didn't think was possible."

"I don't need a lecture."

"I reckon you do Marion. You did the right thing. What they did to the Jews, and the Gypsies  they would do to the world. Africa would be gone; The Japs think they won't turn on the Emperor like they did Stalin but it is a matter of time."

She nodded. "I'm fine."

"No dying embers my dear, this bloody flame must die completely or the Reich will survive. It will return."

"I'm fine, I just wasn't ready for how young he was."

"It was Hitler who killed him ultimately."

It didn't make her feel better. Marion looked back through the door and saw Noah walking back across the field holding two pistols. A Baretta and a Luger. Mallory tapped her on the shoulder. She knew they didn't have time to waste. No more talk, they had to move. Herzog was already in the truck and the engine roared to life. Mallory closed all the blinds and locked the door. He threw the keys away in the tall grass behind the guard house.

Noah picked up his pace and ran back. He lifted himself up a few seconds before Marion. Once they were all in, he pounded on the wall of the cab and they were quickly picking up speed. Marion looked at the casket. Everything was so black and white with Reiter. He was clearly not human. No one could deny that he was a monster.

Mallory moved closer on the bench so he could talk over the roar of the truck and the swirling wind.

"We're in Germany now. Can you handle this?"

Marion nodded. "I can, just need to settle in."

"Marion you've been here for months."

"And all I've done is babysit a monster."

He waved his fingers around "Marion, we are all the monsters tonight."

# CHAPTER
# THIRTEEN

<u>May 1st 11:45 AM: Frankfurt on the southern German pass</u>

NOAH LOOKED at his watch and felt the pressure of time. There were moments when he heard the click of his watch like a metronome. Sometimes it was quiet in the background, and during these long moments of the drive the watch echoed like thunder. He expected to be past Frankfurt by this time. He looked at the map and wondered where Himmler was at this point? It was impossible for him to not think of this as a race.

Marion was first to cover her nose. Noah watched her reaction. There was an intense smell smelling filling the air.

"You smell that?"

Noah knew the smell far too well. Burning city, ash, dust, rotting bodies under rubble for days or longer. The battle of Frankfurt was history for a month now. A bloody house-to-house battle on the streets by day and bombs by night. It was not a short battle but, now it was long over. It was hard to believe the city was still digging itself out.

"Frankfurt?" Mallory asked.

"It was."

"Noah, they know we're coming right?" Herzog yelled from the front.

"Of course."

The occupation of Germany had begun but there were no straight lines. They were driving in and out of Nazi-controlled land, the map said it was Allied-controlled but they had to be prepared for anything. He knew Patrick had given heads up to the commanding Generals Irwin and Grow who had taken the city and held it for the last month. That didn't mean the word had gotten to the outer checkpoints along the highway.

For twenty minutes the smell got stronger and Noah watched the time tick past noon. The truck slowed.

"Good, I can't exactly piss in a bottle like you guys," Marion relaxed her body.

Herzog cursed in German. It was a phrase Noah didn't know. He must have just seen the city. According to the map, they should get a full view of it.

"If there is a bathroom left," Mallory laughed.

"Allied checkpoint!" Herzog yelled before stopping the truck. Noah relaxed and let out a deep breath. Mallory didn't share his calm, his German friend in the driver's seat was still in danger. The truck slowed and the brakes whined a bit as they came to a stop. The sound of boots, American accents, several voices telling him to turn off the truck, machine guns and rifles, all loaded chambers. Then silence, Noah could hear the flow of the nearby river. Herzog had better have his hands up. After a long moment of silence…

"Noah Sandawich?" one of the guards yelled. He comically mispronounced his name like many GIs.

"Did he just call you a sandwich?" Marion said in disbelief. Mallory laughed. It was no longer funny to Noah as many times as it had happened.

"In the back!" Herzog yelled.

"Everybody out. Hands up."

"Sandwich?" Marion whispered at him. Mallory grinned but he was on his feet quickly.

"At least, we know we were expected," Mallory jumped out first and offered to help Marion. She slapped his hands away. Noah stepped out and was shocked. The road wound down through the mountain and the outskirts to the city center. The bridges that connected the two halves of the city were gone.

Some just had a piece missing, others remained stubs on each side of the river bank. The largest remaining structure was an ancient church, only a few buildings were still intact. The city on the southwestern side of the Rhine River was like a drawing thoroughly erased. The destruction was breathtaking to see.

The American soldiers came around the truck. Two privates with rifles and an MP who was a Lieutenant. His uniform said Wilson. He looked impossibly young for an officer. His skin was red and sun burnt, he had freckles. Noah was pretty sure he hadn't seen much sun wherever he grew up.

Behind him, there were teams of Germans picking through the rubble of their homes. Wheelbarrows carried off the larger pieces. Up in the hills, there was less destruction but the work looked daunting. The American troops walked the streets watching with their rifles but they didn't help. Noah didn't feel an ounce of sympathy. Many of the Germans working the piles looked like they had been soldiers.

Wilson held a photo up to Noah's face. He smiled, and Noah relaxed assuming his face matched the photo the young GI had.

"Welcome to Frankfuah…" He wanted to call him by a formal title. He had an accent but Noah couldn't place it yet. The way he said the name of the city was strange, goofy.

"I don't have a rank, Lieutenant. At ease, just call me Noah."

"General Irwin said you were a VIP."

*Boston maybe?* He wasn't sure yet about the accent. Noah appreciated that Patrick stressed the importance of the mission but he didn't want special treatment. "Put your dress uniforms away, we're mud-eaters like you and in a hurry I'm afraid."

Wilson grinned. "You need food or anything?"

Marion raised her hand. "Bathroom?"

One of the privates waved her forward. "The plumbing is blown to shit but we got a bucket and some privacy."

"I'll take it," Marion ran to catch up to the private. "Better than in my pants."

"We had breakfast," Noah realized he hadn't considered lunch. "You got anything besides shingles on hand?"

"Our ham didn't pass the physical, but we'd rather you have it for lunch than the Jerry's."

"Red shit on shingles sounds like lunch," Noah smiled. He

hadn't kept kosher since basic and he doubted whatever spam they brought them would be red, probably as grey as the sky above the city. It would have to do.

Marion came out of the building and scanned the destruction. Noah had seen more than a few ruins during the war, it was her first time seeing a city like this. The Germans near them looked sad and defeated, he worried that she might think too much about that. Noah gave Mallory a look. He walked towards the truck and waved for her to follow. Marion didn't want to follow. Noah smiled for the MP and headed to the truck.

"Excuse me, Noah," Wilson waved him away from the group. "I have no idea what makes you a fat cat with a full pass but I suspect you might know more than a few latrine roomahs."

Noah knew he was sure he was from Boston now.

"Lieutenant, we're in a hurry. Once we get lunch, we're hauling ass east."

Wilson nodded. He was curious but nervous about asking. He had to understand that Noah couldn't tell him more. Noah was curious also.

"Where you from son?"

"Maine, an hour north of Bangah, almost Canada."

Noah held up a finger. "Ahh, I should've guessed that. I'm up north too, Minnesota." The 'where are you from' conversation was always interesting to Noah.

"Hope you don't need to cross the river? We haven't left a bridge whole for miles."

"No, we are staying in the south."

"Careful, the Germans fled to lots of smaller towns and they're wound up as you can imagine."

Noah nodded. But Wilson had more questions.

"Staying south huh? The fighting is up north, is it true the Ruskies took Berlin?"

Noah wondered why these men had no idea. If the Generals were keeping them in the dark for some reason. It was always a cloudy thing considering ethics during war, and everything was changing soon. He believed these men deserved to know the end of the war was nearly here.

"Hitler is dead."

"No shit," Wilson was ecstatic. Before he could celebrate Noah grabbed his arm.

"Tomorrow, they surrender, and eventually they will expect us to forgive them."

Wilson lifted a single eyebrow, his disbelief close to the surface. His hands had the shakes, and in his eyes Noah recognized the thousand-yard stare. This young man had himself a war already. Somewhere between Maine and Frankfurt he'd lost a friend, got hurt, came close to death, or stared into the eyes of evil. Plenty of GIs experienced it all.

"I was at Dacha sir."

Now the pain made sense. Noah gave his arm a reassuring pat. "No Sir here. So you saw it. What they've done."

Wilson was shaken to his core; he didn't need to say it. Noah had wondered if it affected the soldiers who were not Jewish like it had him. The inhumanity was universal. "We had taken this city, we headed straight there behind Patton and his Gasoline Cowboys. We were supposed to set up a hold for the Kraut officers. I heard the talk, but it was different seeing it."

"I was at Ohrdruf, the first one liberated, so I know what you have seen."

Wilson was not a softie but Noah saw the pain, the same that he felt.

"I don't know when they plan to tell you Lieutenant, but for this day, you still have a war to fight you understand me?"

"Loud and clear sir…uh Noah.

Noah saluted him and walked back to the truck. He climbed inside.

"Give 'em hell sir."

Noah turned to get a last look at Wilson. Noah had the thought. He was going home a hero. If he made it through the war. He would never see him again. In the truck, Mallory looked at the spam they had been given. "Blimey. You didn't thank them for this leather, did you?"

Marion tried to chew on it. "Totally leather,"

Noah gave the front cab a smack and the truck came to life with a roar. They had to drive slowly past Frankfurt, the roads were pockmarked, bombed, and scattered with debris.

Noah sat at the back of the truck. He wasn't hungry, he knew he would have to eat but he was enjoying this. He knew he shouldn't, but he felt a certain satisfaction seeing Frankfurt. The road angled down through the city, they had to curve around burned-out German tanks. Many of the buildings were nothing but piles of crushed bricks and boards. The shocked German faces were everywhere, looking not too different from faces begging on the streets after the Great War and the humiliation of the defeat.

Beggars chased the truck. Mallory flipped a piece of bread to a child running after them. He knew much of the population had scattered out of the city. He wanted to tell himself these were the worst of the true believers, but it didn't matter. Germany had called this wrath upon itself.

# CHAPTER
# FOURTEEN

<u>Timeless void of death</u>

IT WAS something deeper than sleep, the dreams something more magical and intense than his human mind had ever created. The souls of those he consumed, their memories, joys, and fears were like a universe to which he was God. Moving like a grain of sand on the wind between their lives. He was more than happy to leave his body behind; it had become a prison. With each year, he was less human and more cursed. He was shackled to the hunger, more intense than anything he experienced in his long life as a human.

He heard the sound of the truck, he knew, even though it was only his second time having this experience. The Nazis he had consumed were the only source of his knowledge and experience with the 20$^{th}$ century. What he knew of this world today was carried to his mind by the blood. He heard the voice of the woman talking to the Jew. He was reduced to a caged creature in a box.

He had been royalty; his brother was on the throne of Wallachia when the Turks came the first time. He was still a child; His brother defended the throne and their lands. He showed the Turks mercy and allowed them to return east. By the time Reiter was a teenager he was given a castle of his own. A pass in the Carpathian Mountains that connected the East and West.

Bethlany Castle sat atop a mountain peak. When his carriage arrived, the bricks were still being laid. The slaves were still carrying furniture up the mountain pass. His brother never forgot how his Reiter fought the Turks, ruthless and cunning at a young age, he was granted the title of Count upon his arrival. The Castle was remote but the tallest spires looked out on the land with unparalleled vistas. It was remote but strategic.

*"You are not banished my brother, you are second in line to the throne, and Bethlany is a shield to protect your rule."*

The Ottoman Empire sent waves of soldiers to capture their lands. They returned with greater force and cruelty. But the Count waited alone in the castle, ready to take the throne upon his brother's death that never came. Battle after battle, stories of his brother being indestructible went around the kingdom as did the tales of cruelty to the Turks. Sadism, gleeful torture, and lips covered with blood it was rumored his brother drank.

The Count grew old hearing the stories. Alone, he watched until the day a carriage finally came up the road. It was late, long after the moon had risen above the forest. It had been years; he had watched himself growing old in the reflections but his brother looked no older as the day they last fought side by side. The Count thought it was a trick of the lamp he held. Something was foul in the oil, it was playing tricks with his mind.

His brother didn't smile only pointed to the door once they'd settled in the library by the dim fire.

*"You've gotten old."*

*"You have not."*

*"Do you fear death brother?"*

The Count considered this question. He didn't fear death, he feared dying here, alone unable to fulfill his destiny.

"The Ottomans will return again, this time they will come for this place. They think their invasion will succeed with this jewel as a base."

"Give me an army."

His brother leaned into the light of the fireplace, his eyes were yellow, like that of a predator. He didn't seem like a man at that moment.

"I will make you an army of one. Forever young and strong. You will never die but there is a cost."

"What cost?"

"Our empire lives only at night; the sun is one of the few weaknesses we have."

"What is the other?"

"Hunger. The curse is blood, fresh human blood, something divine about it we must have or the thin veil with death comes down."

The bargain was explained, but the Count didn't understand what his brother was saying. There was magic and immortality but the hunger was painful, the consumption of souls brought with it a misery that changed him. He was not raised to consider the lives of slaves or peasants. Enemies were only to be destroyed. Now he carried their souls.

He fought off the Turks. They couldn't take his castle and over time, the legend grew. For hundreds of years, he collected the souls of anyone who dared venture near Bethlany. They stopped coming and the land went to seed. He slept; the legend of his monstrosity kept away most invaders. Those who didn't nourish him.

Then came the Great War. No being with his hunger could miss the aura of death that haunted the lands. Then, like the waves of Ottoman invaders, it faded away until the day the Germans came. The legends did nothing to keep them away. The bastards were no different than the Turks who wanted his home to control this castle and in turn his brother's land.

He only wanted to be left alone. The closest fate to death for his body, and living the many lives of his victims or so it felt. The moment German boots stepped onto Bethlany soil and he heard their stomping echo, he had entered the war.

# CHAPTER
# FIFTEEN

May 1st 1:37 PM: Central Germany

ALICE HAD LOST an uncle who worked for the railroad during the first bombing of Leipzig. His body was never found, and no one heard from him after the main rail hub was bombed by the Brits. She thought about him as they approached the outskirts of the city. She moved closer to the back of the truck so she could watch out the back and be closer to Heinrich. He was focused on holding his rifle tight. She wasn't sure he knew she was there until a few minutes ago. He squeezed her leg, and she felt safe just for that moment.

The officer sitting by the outside was eager to give up his seat. It was more exposed. It also meant that she was able to see more of the destroyed buildings and structures. What they could see from the freeway was distressing. The torn-apart rail system bothered her. She'd made the trip by train from Berlin to Munich so many times, always stopping for lunch in Leipzig.

There was a café at the train station her Uncle Peter insisted by. Best strudels in central Germany, the last time they'd sat down there she told him about her new job. She expected him to be proud. He was the only family who wasn't happy for her.

He said "great," but she could tell he wasn't happy. He would never speak badly of the Fuhrer, at the time she wondered why.

Alice looked around the truck and caught Herrmann, an out-of-shape SS officer who'd asked Heinrich twice for a break to piss. As if they could stop the caravan. Each time he was told that we were stopping in Leipzig for fuel. She thought that seeing Goring almost thrown out of the truck might prevent Herrmann from making entitled demands. As far as he was concerned, he was still an officer.

She could see the relief on his face as they slowed down. Sitting closer to the outside she could see there were no buildings anywhere around. It wasn't until the whole caravan stopped that the level of noise was clear to her. She watched the trucks behind them empty along the side of the small two-lane highway.

Heinrich stood up. "We have fifteen minutes to fuel the trucks that are low, whatever business you have to attend to, do it now. No time for modesty I'm afraid."

Herrmann jumped up before he was done speaking. Goring stood up and looked at Heinrich with murder and rage in his eyes. Alice resisted the urge to laugh at these men who couldn't adjust to losing their power. Goring jumped out of the truck. Heinrich didn't look back at Alice before he followed the officers off the truck. They outranked him, but in this situation the command structure had melted. He knew the plan and they didn't. Alice hoped it was enough to keep them safe.

Alice followed him and climbed out into the sun. It was warm for the first of May. She let the sun's rays touch her face and closed her eyes. She didn't realize how long it had been since she had felt its warmth. She had been in a bunker under a city that was covered in smoke. Heinrich kissed her forehead and when she opened her eyes, he had walked off toward a gathering of officers who surrounded Himmler.

The black uniforms almost looked out of place in the sun. Their truck was an anomaly, as it was the only one in the caravan carrying families. Himmler's escape was designed mostly for officers of the SS. They were stretching their legs, a few pissed on trees. Goring marched toward the officers, he intended to complain to Himmler about Henry. Goring suffered from a false sense of his importance. Did he still believe they were winning this war?

Alice felt a little pressure in her bladder but knew her bigger concern was getting water to drink. She followed Irma and her young son towards the tree line where she would squat. She saw Herrmann angrily collecting leaves.

She jogged to catch up to Irma and Josef. The boy had his toy plane in his back pocket and walked with his mother. It occurred to Alice that this was a big risk, leaving and taking her son. Irma must have been afraid to stay in Germany for a good reason. She had taken off her SS pin since they left Berlin.

"Irma, may I ask a question?"

She pointed to a tree and her boy ran to pee on it.

Irma couldn't have been much older than her mid-twenties but she looked like she'd aged since Berlin. Alice offered her a cigarette. She only had five left. No telling when they would get more.

"The Fuhrer let you smoke?"

"Around him?" Alice shook her head. "Only pure Germans fit of..."

"Mind and body can establish a thousand-year Reich." Irma took the cigarette. Alice flipped open her lighter and they enjoyed their first drags. Alice took the smoke into her lungs, closed her eyes and enjoyed the brief dizzy light-headed feel.

BANG. The gunshot echoed in the distance, all the people pissing in the woods turned to look but they couldn't see beyond the trucks. Alice almost jumped out of her skin. She had a strong feeling she knew who it was.

"Goring," Alice said.

Irma nodded. "No time for his behavior."

"Where is your husband?"

Irma looked away and then shook her head. "Died for the Fatherland just after we were married, before..." she got choked up. She pointed at her son.

"He was SS, worked in Warsaw for the occupation authority, a Jew dog surprised him, left him bleeding in a gutter."

"You're in the SS?"

Irma nodded. "Frauenkorps, Communication, and translation, but I was not good at it. So, they transferred me."

"Where?"

Irma didn't seem to want to talk about it. "Have you heard of Auschwitz?"

Alice had not. Josef ran to his mother and hugged her, she bent down to kiss his head. Horns blared. They needed to return to the trucks. They walked back, Irma tapped her son's shoulders to move him faster.

"I have not heard of Auschwitz."

Irma flicked the cigarette. "Good, it is better you have not."

Alice had a feeling now. It was one she had buried deep when the Allies first crossed into their land. The Fuhrer even in private denied the camps. He told her personally that the Americans were lying to justify their invasion. In the last days, she heard him blame Himmler, then in a letter she typed for him, he said history would remember them for eradicating the Jewish filth. She knew then that the rumors were true.

As she walked back to the truck, many had already loaded up. She saw his body. Goring was slumped in a pile. She wondered what he had said, what message Himmler was sending. Heinrich waited at the truck, his hand out. He helped Irma and her son in first.

Alice took his hand and for a moment she thought about not getting in the truck. She just typed letters. She didn't do the awful things these men did. Perhaps her son could grow up in a new Germany. Heinrich's hand felt warm in hers. She didn't want to raise this boy without a father.

She looked around for a moment at the caravan. They wouldn't just leave her here. She would remain forever with Goring. Worse, in her heart, she knew the world would destroy Germany forever. Their only hope was to rebuild elsewhere.

"Let's go my love."

For Germany, she thought and got back in the truck. For my son.

# CHAPTER
# SIXTEEN

May 1ˢᵗ 4:17 PM: Berchtesgaden, German Alps

MARION INSTINCTIVELY REACHED for her Ruby. Her hand fumbled with the pistol before she realized it was Mallory giving her a shake. Her holster was still clipped shut.

"Wakey, wakey."

"Where? How long?"

Marion sat up. The truck was still speeding down a two-lane highway as she looked out the open back. She shook her head as if she could shake off the haze of sleep. Her watch read four something, her eyes couldn't focus on the thinner minute hand.

"Berchtesgaden," said Noah. "Any minute now."

Marion was surprised she had fallen asleep, let alone that she was soundly out for several hours. Mallory had told her often that in war you sleep whenever and wherever you can. It was then that she noticed the thinner, colder air.

The Brit sat giving her a skeptical look. "It appears to still be a Nazi town for the moment, you prepared to act German?"

Marion nodded, despite how afraid she really was inside. Mallory took a deep breath and smiled. He saw right through her. She knew it.

"I'm fine."

Mallory smiled, "Mir geht es gut, danke."

Noah opened the hatch to the front cab. "You know where you are going?"

Herzog held up his thumb and focused on the road. Noah sat back down and could only wait with the rest of them. They were meeting a double agent, one that Mallory had worked with before. Someone he trusted. A Nazi who had betrayed the party long ago. Marion didn't know if this man realized that Hitler was crazy, wrong or that he simply couldn't win. Either way, he was helping them.

The truck slowed down and they prepared. Marion unclipped the holster that held Ruby. Noah lowered the hat over his face. His Semitic features might as well be a Jewish star on his sleeve. They stopped at a checkpoint and someone yelled at them in German. They sat still as an SS guard with an MG 42 rifle came around and looked in the back of the truck. He looked at the coffin.

Herzog spoke in German to the checkpoint commander. Marion's rough grasp of German only helped her to catch bits and pieces. Funeral home, hero of the Fatherland and his children. All from the agreed-upon story.

Marion decided to smile at the young guard, but he didn't smile back. He stared at Noah. Mallory kept his eyes on the guard. Marion worried that the stare was too much, making the guard suspicious. The guard couldn't see Mallory's hands from his position. Marion could, she watched him inching toward his pistol. Before he got there, there was a tap on the hood.

The truck revved to life, and they rolled away. Mallory waved at the guard. Noah breathed a sigh of relief.

"That was close," Marion whispered. No one else seemed as worried as she was.

From the back of the truck, she saw snowcapped mountains and a river as blue as the clearest sky. She had only been asleep for two hours, but looking at this small village you would think the war had happened in another world. The buildings were intact, mixed into the trees and built into the sides of the mountain, the Nazi flags still fluttered in the breeze. As they passed through the town, they got a look at the beautiful lake that swelled with melted snow this time of year.

She saw a group of teenagers diving in the lake one after another.

It was beautiful. It was sad to think of the tranquility being broken but it seemed the war was coming to this place. They drove just past the entrance to the funeral home. Herzog backed up the truck so that when they took the coffin inside, they would be quick.

The door to the funeral home opened and a woman stepped out. She was in her thirties, brown shirt and uniform pants. Nazi armband, but the blonde woman had her hair beautifully curled under a beret. She was stunning, her beauty a strange contrast to the ugly symbol on her arm. When they stopped Mallory jumped out. He kissed this woman on the cheek and spoke in German.

"Your father Hans returns to the Fatherland."

The woman gripped a tissue, her tears appeared real enough. *Was this woman the double agent?* She smiled at Mallory for just a heartbeat and then slipped back into the role of grief-stricken daughter. Two guards waited by the doors. A crowd had gathered on the street. A few of the younger people in the crowd extended their arms in salute, like proud Nazis they honored the fallen. Herzog came around and waited as Noah and Marion pushed the coffin out.

Marion watched the late afternoon sun hit the outside of the coffin. Herzog and Mallory lifted the corners and waited for Noah and Marion to jump down. Once they had the weight in their hands the German woman held the door open for them. As they entered the building there was applause outside. When the door finally shut, they all felt a sense of relief. She was the double agent for sure, she locked the door behind her. She and Mallory shared a long hug. Marion never saw Mallory as anything more than a kindly Uncle, or a brother in arms. Something about the affection he was showing this woman made her uncomfortable. It wasn't jealousy, it was a mystery and sight of the armband. The two stayed in each other's arms speaking softly.

Marion struggled to hold the casket and scanned the funeral home with her eyes. At the far end of the room was a large open window that looked out over the small town, the lake, and the snowcapped mountain. It was a stunning view, and another day she would have enjoyed it. As beautiful as it was it was also an impossibly perfect strategic spot.

"Perfect," Noah whispered.

They couldn't enjoy the view just yet, Marion  strained to hold the weight of the monster, but she didn't want to be the first to complain. They lowered the coffin into the sanctuary. Each of them caught their breath. The woman walked into the room. Mallory's smile was puppy dog-like, it was clear as glass there was something between them. It might not be romantic but they were happy to see each other.

"Anke, meet the team."

Anke nodded at the introductions. Marion sighed, she didn't trust this woman and it seemed a mistake to use their real names. Noah must've been thinking the same because he looked at her with hatred visible in his clenched fists and tightening jaw.  The two locked eyes and it was uncomfortable for everyone. Mallory stepped between them and stared at Noah.

He looked at Noah but spoke to the room. "You can trust her; she saved my life."

"And he saved mine," her voice was as cold as a winter morning. "I have no love for the Fuhrer, what he did to this nation, to our people. I'll do anything to defeat him."

"Good news..." Mallory smiled.

Noah put up his hand to stop him. "The good news is our mission is crucial to defeating him."

Marion and Mallory shared a look. So, Noah didn't want her knowing the big man's skull was in Soviet hands being checked against dental records.

Noah looked around. "What about this place?"

Anke spoke in English. "Paid for, the owner of the funeral home will not return until morning."

"The guards?" Noah asked.

"They're hers," Mallory insisted.

She nodded. Mallory grabbed her hand. "I'm surprised. How many suicide missions can one Limey survive?"

"Let's hope you didn't curse him," Herzog added.

Mallory laughed. Anke looked down at the coffin. "Do I want to know who is in there?"

"That's the curse right there."

They all shared a look. Noah grinned. "That is need to know I'm afraid."

Anke raised an eyebrow. "I suppose you want to see the equipment."

"Did you get enough rope?"

She laughed, "What are we doing? Climbing to the Eagle's nest?"

No one answered, and Mallory grinned.

"You can't be serious." Anke was stunned, "after dark, we can hike the road, it takes a few hours…"

"They will mine that road, hide guards." Noah pointed to the main room. "We have a plan."

They walked into the main room of the funeral parlor. It really was an oddly perfect spot. The village center was behind them and out of sight. They wouldn't be able to see the Reich headquarters in town, but the rest of the view was too perfect. Through the big window, they could see the highway the Nazis would come in on. They would turn onto the same road 15 KM back they had come in on. They would wind up these roads, come around the lake and cross the last bridge before the nest and then drive up the winding road to the Alpine Fortress. They couldn't really see the fortress at this distance with the naked eye but with the telescope, the view was perfect.

Noah was first to carefully lean down and look through the telescope. "There it is." He waved Mallory to stand next to him. Marion was last to look. She was surprised at how clear it was in the eyepiece. It was the size of a castle but with modern construction.

Noah leaned over and gave it a longer look. "When is local sunset?"

"Seven-thirty or so," Anke reflexively looked at her watch.

"Assault begins at eight." Noah looked back toward the coffin in the sanctuary. "We need wait to make sure they arrive and then get as close as we can before dark."

"We can park on the far side of the lake, there is a path through the woods. But the truck can only make it so far…"

Noah put up his hand. "Get us as close as you can."

"Long way to be pallbearers," Marion hated to point out the obvious but no one else was saying it.

Anke was confused, "Is it a bomb?"

"If only my dear," Mallory shook his head. "If only."

# CHAPTER
# SEVENTEEN

MALLORY THREW a handful of water on his face. The feeling of the cold water was refreshing, he wished he had time to swim in the lake but this would have to do. He looked at his face in the tiny bathroom mirror as he dried it with a hand towel. It was unbelievable that he was still alive.

He felt old and damned lucky to have lived through two wars. He was used to the baby faces of this war. It was hard to believe he had been as young as them in the first one. It was sad that these nations sent their young people to fight these battles. Countless souls who never grew old, dying for lines on a map. Early in this war, he had waved off the misery of the young lads. He would tell them of the trenches and explain what real horror was. He was angered by the Blitz, motivated to keep his boys out of the war and then he saw the horrors of the Nazis. It was almost hard to fathom the cruelty of these monsters. He went quickly from self-interest to righteous fury.

There was a knock at the door. Mallory didn't feel like talking. He needed this moment. He needed strength for one last night. The second knock was more insistent. He hoped this was the final time he performed this ritual.

"Just a minute," Mallory said and straightened his hair. He watched his doubt and fear melt away in the mirror. He unlatched the door and it opened so quickly he was afraid he was being attacked. He started for his pistol and saw it was Anke. He smiled as she pushed him back in and latched the door in a single motion.

"They're going to think we're lovers my dear."

"You wish."

"Why Anke, I am a happily married man." He was amused. She was clearly not.

"I don't care what your team thinks."

Mallory was speechless for the moment, being this close to her made him uncomfortable.   He would be lying if he ignored the effect she had on him. Nonetheless, they had a complicated and intense history. She had smuggled him out of Bulgaria after he managed to steal the plans for a U-boat offensive against the Royal and US Navies. She had killed her own guards and offered to be a double agent. She wanted a promise of amnesty after the war. He promised her only a phone call with Field Marshal Brunner, head of special operations. They hiked for seventy-two hours across occupied lands. She sold the SS a story that she and her team were tracking him. If the Partisans had found them, she was in as much danger as he was from Germans. They huddled together at night for warmth, he was fond of her but she made clear the intimacy was pure survival. She was an amazing woman, he wasn't sure he could have resisted if she had wanted more.

Once he was clear he gave her a black eye and stabbed her for effect. She returned to the Nazis and by all accounts, Brunner said she remained an asset.

"What is the good news the Je...Noah wouldn't tell me?"

Mallory couldn't help but notice she came very close to calling Noah the Jew. Noah was holding back the news of Hitler's death for a reason, he suspected that she wouldn't help them if the surrender of her country was so close. But she'd given him a perfect way to change the subject.

"What did you almost call him?"

Anke rolled her eyes. "I have spent four years playing the role of an officer. So, my tongue slipped."

Mallory understood, he did. It was confusing being a spy. The lines were so blurred they were meaningless. "Noah is a serious man of faith, and fierce. You make that mistake around him and you'll regret it."

"Himmler knows who he is, trust me on that."

She talked with Himmler. Mallory knew Anke was a rare beauty anywhere, but in that uniform, with her racial purity. Himmler being a married man meant nothing. As disgusting as it would be for her, she would never turn down drinks with the Reichsführer of the Schutzstaffel. This is the kind of valuable information that comes out of moments like that.

"How well does Himmler know him?"

"He has pictures in his office, taken in France, he knows his name, and where his family lives in the States. He called him Die furchterregende Ratte."

Mallory laughed. "I do think Noah will like that, the fearsome part."

"Maybe he is no better than them?"

Mallory raised an eyebrow. "War is ugly my dear, you know that." He could've asked her about the guards she killed to free him. Men she worked with, with families. He didn't need to say it. He could see it under the surface. Her eyes said everything.

"What didn't he want me to know?" Anke pulled him closer into her arms. She thought she could change the subject. He guessed that she had used this trick for survival many times. Mallory wished for a moment this was real, that she wasn't playing him. She whispered, her lips close to his. "Tell me please."

There was a time he may have melted. He had nowhere to retreat. "Anke, I have a question for you."

"Anything," She whispered, her lips closer. He wasn't fool enough to believe that she really had any desire to kiss him. He didn't blame her either, all is fair in love and war. He knew this was about the latter.

"What do you think should happen to them after the war? Hitler, Himmler, and Goebbels."

She stepped back, her face changed. The distraction had failed and her face turned back to ice. "I suppose they must stand trial. The Russians won't allow it, but I trust your country and America. They must face justice."

"Courts?"

She nodded.

Mallory leaned closer. He was still close enough to smell her hair. "Don't tell Noah, if I tell you." Anke smiled again. She should've understood the spell was broken, but he rubbed her shoulder gently to give her the impression that he was weak to her powers. Then he lied through his teeth. "The SS elite are gathering at the Eagle's Nest to plan an assault with a new weapon. Much deadlier than the V2 against Moscow."

"Fools."

Mallory nodded. "They have to die Anke, you understand that don't you."

"If the Russians take Berlin, the Fuhrer will have no choice but surrender."

"They're here!" They heard Noah's faint voice through the door.

Mallory stepped out. He went down the long hall and heard Anke's heels behind him.

The rest of the team was gathered at the window, their attention taken by something happening in town. No one saw Mallory and Anke step out of the Bathroom together. Noah had binoculars, Marion and Herzog both stood behind him. Mallory reached into his pack and pulled out his own binoculars. It was hard to see at first because the trees blowing in the mountain wind covered each side of the road. They were focused on the clearing near the lakeside. The first vehicle came around the bend. An open Jeep with a machine gunner strapped in and a Nazi flag blowing in the breeze. A truck, like the one they rode in, another. Truck after truck.

"Jesus H. Christ," Marion whispered. "They keep coming."

Mallory stopped counting Nazis and watched Noah's face carefully. Noah's hands tightened on his binoculars as the sheer number of them became clear. They suspected there would be this many, but it was another thing to see them all arrive. Noah was happy, Actually excited. The more the merrier. Mallory looked back at the sanctuary and the coffin and silently he agreed.

# CHAPTER
# EIGHTEEN

May 1ˢᵗ 5:15 PM: Berchtesgaden, German Alps

THE CROWDS LINED the street as they passed by, they cheered and put their arms out in salute. Alice watched in amazement. She wondered if the people of this mountain village had any idea that the Fuhrer was dead and that the Soviets had captured the Capital. Here in the mountains after their long drive, it was like the war didn't exist.

Behind the crowd, she saw the beautiful clear water of the lake. For the first time, her Heinrich relaxed and dropped his rifle. He reached out and held her hand. She felt relief at his touch and a wave of sorrow at the same time. She knew this was the last time she would see or feel Germany as it was. She wished they could stop the truck and freeze time. Stay in Berchtesgaden forever.

"We made it, we're safe now." Heinrich smiled at her.

The mountain wind blew her hair wildly, she assumed after hours in the truck that she looked like a mess. She gripped his hand. She wasn't sure this world would ever let them feel safe. Herrmann and Irma were celebrating, they certainly felt more confident than her. She looked outside as they turned just before the city center. They passed a community center, a few cafes, and the local funeral home before the caravan turned onto the road that snaked along the lake.

"Once we are on the mountain, no one can stop us." He assured her. "I have one thing left to do."

They stared out at the lake. The snow-capped peaks were reflected in the clear surface. When she looked up at the mountain she remembered coming here with Eva. So many meetings with the Fuhrer who loved being here more than anywhere else in the Fatherland. They came on a bus that felt bigger than the windy road. They held each other's hands as they climbed higher and higher. Berchtesgaden itself felt high above the world but the cold thin air of the Eagle's nest was hard to explain. The bus almost overheated making the climb.

She was not alone in asking where they were going, but no one in their trucks had answers. She suspected Heinrich knew but chose not to tell her. She decided to respect that.

Heinrich went to the box that he and stronger men had loaded in the tunnel outside of Berlin. Little Josef looked inside the box. Heinrich told him to be careful.

"Are there mines in that box?"

Heinrich grinned. "No, but that is a great question son. There will be a Jeep laying the mines, but we have an important job."

The truck turned onto a long bridge that crossed the river coming down from the peak. The trucks in front of them were already making the climb. When they crossed the bridge they pulled to the side of the road, there were several roars as the trucks behind them flew past.

Heinrich grabbed the large case; he strained a bit with the weight of it and jumped out. Alice couldn't help but lean out to watch him. A Jeep with a large machine gun mounted in the back had pulled to the other side of the road. She watched the soldier dig a hole quickly and the gunner drop a metal device in the hole. Landmines.

Heinrich put the large case directly in the center of the bridge. There was a large gust of wind. Even from this distance, she could see him stop and close his eyes to enjoy the breeze.

"Come on! Come on!" The driver yelled at him from the front cab. Alice never saw what their driver looked like. Heinrich opened the case, reached in, and armed the bomb. She only guessed, but he ran like it was actually about to blow. He avoided the mine and grabbed the back of the truck as it sped away. Alice pulled him in.

"Everyone heads down, cover your ears!"

# CHAPTER
# NINETEEN

PERHAPS IT WOULD HAVE BEEN EASIER if the Russians had found them along the way. If a stray bomb took out their caravan. If Noah was being honest with himself, he would admit that he was happy that Himmler had made it this far. He wanted this more than anything since the war began. All his anger and sorrow had been directed to this moment and making sure these bastards didn't escape. He knew they were feeling pretty good about their chances. There were a lot of Nazis going up that mountain, but he trusted his plan.

Noah watched them, couldn't take his eyes off them. His binoculars were strong enough that he could watch all their movements. The SS soldier carried the case out to the middle of the bridge and paused for a moment before setting the explosive.

"Here it goes..." Mallory whispered.

The last truck and Jeep peeled out but they could only build so much speed going up the mountain road. If he didn't watch the bridge explode, if they didn't know better they could easily have mistaken the blast for thunder. The sound and shockwave rolled across the lake; it rattled the windows of the mountain village slightly.

Marion sighed deeply. "It's on."

Anke shook her head. "You'll never scale that mountain."

Mallory laughed. "'*You'll never*' are words that have never stopped us before."

"We have a trick up our sleeve," Noah watched the flames that had been the bridge fall into the river. He hoped she wouldn't ask. "Load the truck, we leave in five."

# CHAPTER
# TWENTY

ALICE GRIPPED the bench tightly with her left hand and Heinrich squeezed her right. Heinrich kept an eye on his watch. The truck engine whined as the driver gunned it, fighting against the steep grade, the Jeep behind them was almost at their bumper. Heinrich silently counted. She watched his mouth as he counted down, her hands already over her ears.

"Heads down!" Heinrich let go of the truck and covered his ears, Alice buried one ear into his chest and covered her other ear.

The universe ignited. The bomb swallowed the bridge with an impossible boom. It was as if a massive clap of thunder was rattling the marrow in their bones as the explosion shook the truck. She kept her head against Heinrich, and even with the warning, it triggered the feeling and memory in her of the bombs dropping on Berlin. There was a shockwave, like an earthquake that traveled across the land shaking everything. Alice felt it punch her in the chest. She screamed involuntarily, in her mind the heat and flames were consuming them. It was a searing heat that nipped the truck.

She looked back down the hill. The flames had mostly shot

straight up, sparing them. The bridge fell apart into three major pieces crashing into the river with another loud boom. The Jeep pulled aside to place more mines. No one could follow them. If they somehow got across to the road, it would be littered with mines.

"We're safe now," Heinrich announced to everyone in the truck. Many faces nodded back. Alice watched the respect on the face of young Josef. The relief of his mother. Herrmann finally opened his eyes. Alice didn't feel safe yet because she had been on this road before.

Heinrich leaned down and kissed her sweat and soot-streaked forehead. He whispered, just for her. "We're safe now."

"I hate this road," Alice yelled at Heinrich, but over the struggling engine of the truck and the echo of the bomb, he didn't even hear her. He had never been here. Only the highest-ranking members of the party and Hitler's inner circle ever saw the Eagle's Nest. It was a beautiful sanctuary that she always felt the Fuhrer deserved, but this road consistently filled her with terror.

It was thin, barely enough for one car, let alone a truck or bus. It was dirt and gravel; the rocks were thicker on the edges just before the drop-off. Whenever the truck edged closer to the sides of the narrow parts of the road, you could hear the rocks spitting up over the edge. The fear caused her stomach to drop and grit her teeth every time, sure they were about to go down the side of the mountain to a painful death. Her heart beat faster as they slowed to climb up to the sky. Irma's joy at the prospect of escape melted away as the grade was fifteen percent, she hugged her boy as their luggage slid back into the straps holding them down.

Alice felt like she was going to slip out. Heinrich's grip on her hand tightened, she enjoyed the vice-like feeling on her hand, she hoped he'd never let go. The mix of her ears popping, and the echo of the bomb gave her a disconnected feeling. It all felt strange, with the burning bridge becoming more distant and the air growing colder. The truck almost felt like it would tip backwards. Since they were the last truck in the caravan, there were several new tears in the truck's protective cloth made by flying pieces of shrapnel from the bridge which let in a breeze that cut like a knife. They were lucky, the shrapnel could have hurt someone. She looked through the hole as they turned corners she saw other trucks ahead, working up the hill. They all struggled to climb.

For twenty minutes they pushed slowly up the hill. They got a surreal view of the orange dot in the sky when they circled the west side of the mountain. The sun had an orange glow because of the smoke that rose across all of Europe. It was the ashes of Germany making the sun glow that beautiful orange. The burning buildings, the scorched earth, and the bodies of those who died for the Fatherland. She felt shame at enjoying the view even for a moment.

She felt anger surge inside her, it was so unfair. She felt her belly and her son. That hurt her heart, she thought about the sacrifices Heinrich and all like him had made. The heartache the Fuhrer felt when the world rejected his vision. She wiped away tears thinking that her boy would never claim his birthright.

They had to be close. She looked out the back of the truck. Berchtesgaden was far enough away that it looked tiny. They turned off the road and everyone breathed a sigh of relief. The truck pulled alongside the row of parked trucks. Heinrich helped her out.

The trucks were lined up beside the airstrip, giving just enough space for the wings of the plane. Two of the trucks moved to block the end of the road. Alice looked out at the peaks of the Alps and it was easy to forget about the rest of the world, the war, and all the sad things happening in the world. Heinrich gripped her shoulders, as the SS officer shot the tires of the truck.

"Wow," little Josef had just seen the building. The size of two football pitches with towers and spires that touched the heavens, the Alpine Fortress would have been a magnificent sight anywhere, but here with the backdrop of the endless-looking snowcapped Alps, it was breathtaking. Among the gathered officers, the reaction was the same, astonishment.

Heinrich gathered everyone from their truck. "Don't get too comfortable, you'll get a room key at the entrance, get what rest you can, we leave after midnight."

"Leave?" Herrmann was beside himself. "Where can we go?"

"What, did you think we could hide here forever?" Irma was annoyed.

"The planes will land here," Heinrich pointed to the airstrip. "They will take us to the new Fatherland in Manchuria."

"Landing here is madness," Herrmann sounded defeated.

Heinrich nodded. "We have little choice."

"We could surrender still, throw ourselves on the mercy of the Americans, this far south…"

"Stop!" Irma the kind-hearted mother disappeared. A harsher person with the same face stared back at them suddenly. "Some of us can expect no mercy."

Alice wasn't sure she fully understood, but it seemed that Irma had a deeper fear of justice. She said she had been a guard at a camp for Jews. She knew the Allies were spreading lies about the camps, in an attempt to turn the world against them. Alice smiled at Irma's little boy. "If we are to rebuild the Fatherland, one day we'll take Germany back from the devils, but we must continue to sacrifice."

Heinrich took her hand, he was proud of her and she felt it coming off him. She shivered from the cold, the only comfort she had was her Henry. Alice didn't know if she really believed, but Irma nodded before leading her son toward the building. Herrmann remained unconvinced. He made a show of storming off.

This left Heinrich and Alice alone on the airstrip. He stared at her as the wind blew through her hair. He leaned down and they shared a kiss.

"It shouldn't have ended like this," she whispered before tearing up. She believed so deeply in the Fuhrer. The world didn't understand. They never saw him with Eva, with Blondie. With her. He was a powerful man, and he had challenged the world. If only the world could understand how far they came so quickly. They just needed to clean the world of the filth and make it pure. They could have made the world strong like Germany.

"We have everything we need here Alice. Here on this

mountain is the future. We can and will rebuild. The Reich is not dead. Our son will grow old in the Reich I promise."

She closed her eyes and tried to picture it.

An officer whistled and waved them from the landing strip. "Find your rooms, get some rest."

Alice and Heinrich walked hand in hand to the future of the Reich.

# CHAPTER
# TWENTY-ONE

May 1st 6:15 PM: Lake Berchtesgaden

NOAH CLIPPED and unclipped his holster multiple times, he was ready to go. The bumpy ride they endured told him they had gone off the road that circled the lake. They were on some kind of mountain road. The light outside the truck had decreased as they were in the woods under thick tree cover. Mallory managed to close his eyes and relax. Anke was upfront directing Herzog. Marion had a stoic look but he knew she had to be a bundle of nerves. She was new to war, only a few hours removed from her first kill. Worse, they were close to sticking their heads in the lion's mouth.

The truck slowed, the shaking intensified and suddenly they stopped. Herzog gunned the engine, but even without looking Noah knew they had gone as far as they could. The wheels spun and mud flew in the air. Mallory pounded on the front cab.

"Stop, the bloody truck we're stuck"

Noah jumped out and looked around to get his bearings. They were deep in the woods past the lake. The sun was bright, whatever smoke that floated off of the war hugged the lower elevations, and now the sun trickled through the leaves blowing in the wind. It was dipping in the west; nighttime would come quickly when the sun went below the horizon. He wondered when or how they would know Reiter was safe. *Would faint light through trees or over the horizon be enough to kill him?*

They wouldn't open the box until they were sure.

Noah turned to look at the back wheels of the truck, the center bolt was deep under the thick mud. Noah looked up, they were on the mountain, too close to look up and see the Eagle's Nest. They were closer than he expected. Anke and Herzog came to look at it. Mallory hung his legs out of the back of the truck as if sitting on a dock.

"The truck is bollocks now," Mallory shook his head.

Noah didn't even look back. "Don't be such a dead battery, Mallory."

Marion stepped out of the truck and her stunned look hid nothing. "How far are we carrying the Count?"

"It's getting dark soon," Herzog added.

Noah was frustrated with their complaints. "You all going to bang your gums all day or get to work?"

Mallory jumped down and stood face-to-face with his old friend. "Ready when you are sir." Mallory saluted him.

"You wanted to be at the rockface before dark, we better go." Anke walked up the path, she was making clear that she was guiding them, not helping carry. Each of them had to wear a heavy length of rope wrapped around their bodies. The length when connected would get them up the bluff, without the heavy ropes they were getting nowhere. Noah felt the weight of the rope and braced himself for the complaints. Each one of the team reacted to the heavy feeling of the ropes with grunts and no words. He didn't want to hear it, so he was glad when they all quietly accepted it.

The hard work had not even started. Mallory tugged on the coffin until he and Herzog could balance it on the ropes over their shoulder. They walked forward, Noah and Marion got into position to put the back corner of the coffin on their shoulders. When the weight came off the truck, he heard Marion grunt slightly. It felt heavy on his shoulder but the rope buffered some of the pressure. They would have to take breaks as the ropes slowly dug into their shoulders.

"OK, blokes we need a rhythm now, watch my steps" Mallory walked carefully, the group followed him stepping carefully. Anke walked ahead on the trail. They couldn't talk, needing to concentrate on their steps. Despite the struggle and hard work of it all, the sounds of nature were beautiful. The lake spilled into the river, the birds sang. It was hard to believe the war was coming to this mountain. He wished they could enjoy it.

Through the trees, they could look up and see the rockface of the final bluff. The sun directly lit the mountain, and above, out of sight, was the Eagle's Nest. Three hundred feet straight-up of rock was the last insurmountable barrier to the Nazi compound. If they got past it, then they would be able to walk up the last peak like a light hike. That rock wall and the mined road gave the scumbags a sense of safety. He wondered *are they drinking? Celebrating their escape? Planning their Far East Fatherland?*

Noah felt the rage surge in him again. Still, they had another hour or so of slow-walking the coffin. It was a painful walk but the rage drove him to keep walking. He was glad no one complained.

They walked for several minutes which felt like hours until they came to a clearing. They had to step through tall blades of grass almost to their knees that blew in the wind. Noah first felt the wind on his face and then the rays of the sun on the side of his face. For a moment the heat rose, and sweat formed every-where on his body. It was uncomfortable. The glowing orange sun was just over the mountains to the west. For the moment, the smoke had cleared and the sun shined directly on them as they walked toward the west. Even the wood of the box had warmed up.

# CHAPTER
# TWENTY-TWO

<u>The void of death</u>

THE FIRST THING he felt was the warming air. The sensation of heat created by the sun warmed the composite lumber of his coffin. He floated still in darkness, safe from the killing power of the light even as the heat oozed through the cracks and into the void of his slumber. In the dreams of death, the memory, and the experiences of his victims live on. He picked from every life he consumed, their dreams became his. Each soul was a universe to explore, but the warmth of objective reality crept into the box and nipped at his flesh. The slight heat boring into the wood of his coffin meant one thing, the sun was shining directly on the coffin. He was inches from oblivion, a state he often considered.

For Reiter the hours awake were just biological function, feeding was a task that was only fuel for the undeath. In the physical world, he had evolved past the human, a perfect hunter for the shadows. Living the lives of those he had taken, for better or for worse. He relived the joy and love at will and only unleashed the cruelty and brutality when required. He kept the evil coiled inside, he was not a heartless creature.

He felt the last rays of the sun. He could feel it shrinking. When Earth spun towards darkness, dusk pulled him to wake, the blood moved differently as night fell. It called on his body to live again, to embrace the coming night and leave the chains of death. Blood called to him.

His eyes opened to the darkness of the coffin. He felt the motion of the outside world. The heat of the dying light. He could not live yet. They were carrying him; he could hear them struggling, but he also felt clearly how they were overworking their bodies. Hearts pounding heavy, he smelled the blood; he could sense it traveling around their bodies. Their hearts pumped harder. He read their blood like an open book.

One of them walked ahead of the rest. He hadn't met her, but he knew she was a German, he felt the power of guilt seeping out of her pores. Waves of it poured off of her so powerful it traveled to his nose. It was not unlike Samvovich's rage, he wore it like armor, and carried it like a weapon, forged in the memory of the horrors he witnessed. Mallory's rage was deeper, but it was there. Herzog's fear of the past haunted him, he did things for the Reich that he would never admit to his friends. He was nervous around Samvovich.

They judged him a monster, but the war was in their souls. They were all killers, now even Riverwood, whose violence was fresh. Whatever she had done had changed her. Her anger towards him was more dangerous than when Reiter had laid down in this box.

The German was different, she wasn't working nearly as hard, yet still her heart raced and her guilt felt overpowering and immediate, similar to Riverwood's fresh murder. They shouldn't trust Reiter, he didn't know why they did. They really shouldn't.

Despite their judgment of him, he was committed to destroying the Nazis and completing the mission. They were right to fear him, if he changed his mind, they couldn't stop him. He would fight instinct when he could. Yet this German, he didn't understand why they seemed to trust her. He was ready, in all the centuries that he hunted he had never uncoiled all the death and cruelty he had consumed. It was in him, something he never felt the need to unleash. He finally understood why he kept these feelings inside. He found the monsters deserving and now they would pay.

# CHAPTER
# TWENTY-THREE

ALICE SAT in the deep chair at the window as tall as the room watching the sunset over the Alps. Built over the edge of the peak, it was the most stunning vista in all the Fatherland. Even after the drive, the isolation of four months spent in the bunker affected her. The view didn't feel real. The chair was so big, her feet didn't touch the floor. The comfort was not just the soft chair, but the memory she had of it. There were two chairs facing the window with its endless-looking view atop the world.

She looked at the empty chair beside her and thought of her friend Gerda. It was like her ghost was there. She had stayed behind in the bunker. Boorman had recruited Gerda to be in Hitler's secretary pool years before Alice. Gerda remained a party member even after her first husband gave his life in North Africa. The Fuhrer himself saw to match her with her second marriage, Erick was a driver. Not as handsome as her first husband but a safe choice. Close to the Fuhrer, in his trusted circle just as Gerda was. They never left him. Erick and Gerda were at the celebration after taking Poland, and Paris. Gerda poured drinks for El Duce and Franco, and she was there beyond the bitter end.

But it wasn't until this moment that she wondered what had happened to her friend. Magda had told her husband that he was the chancellor. They all heard the bullet; they all knew he was dead but when Magda said those words to Goebbels it was just as hard to hear. Gerda clutched her tissues and ran out of the room. Erick ran after her and in all the chaos it wasn't until she saw the empty chair here in the Eagle's Nest that Alice realized she would never see her again. Alice watched sunlight shine through the window on the empty chair. She and Gerda came and sat in these chairs often, day and night when the generals and commanders wanted the Fuhrer to attend to the war. They stayed and waited in case the Fuhrer called them back.

They sat here on the last night of August in 1939 after the Fuhrer gave General Franz Halder the order to invade Poland. They sat here the first night of the Blitz, watching the sun go down knowing their planes were almost across the channel. The Fuhrer had insisted their entourage return to Berlin, but his council wanted him safe out of the city if the British returned fire. It was some time that week that Gerda typed up the cable to hurry the construction of the Berlin bunker.

It had been a clear sunset that evening so early in the war just as it was tonight. Alice wished she could prop the sun up longer, she knew it was not just dropping on the Alps but the war and the Reich. The officers argued behind her as she watched the sunlight fade against the chair. She was so small against the big chair; she was sure they didn't know she was there. The weight of it hit her. *Where was Gerda? Did the Russians or the Americans have her? What would they do to her?*

She felt a pang of guilt at being here, on the verge of escape. So many Germans would not escape.

Behind her at the large table, the men in their black, perfectly pressed uniforms argued. She didn't want to hear them begging.

"No number system, the first planes need to prioritize the ranking officers."

"Women and children should be on the first plane."

"The Soviets killed Boorman."

"The Allies are not accepting the surrender."

"They already accepted it. The war is over, we can throw ourselves at the mercy…"

"There is no mercy, don't be a fool."

It went on and on. She didn't pay attention until she heard Heinrich.

"This not how we start a new Fatherland, we must stand together now more than ever. The Americans, the Soviets, Jews, the Slavs, and all the other filth that feared us have won this round, but we will live to fight another day—only if we work together. My Alice and I will prove our faith we'll wait until the last plane is out."

Alice felt her stomach drop, fear creeped over her. She closed her eyes, she couldn't believe they were still debating their right to be here.

"That is brave Mister Hitzinger," It was Himmler.

Heinrich assured him. "I am taking command, I will make sure everyone, every German on this mountain makes it to the new Fatherland."

Himmler was detestable. Of course, he was willing to let Henry stay and command the last mission. A man who for years wielded such power and did so brutally was right to fear the world would show him no mercy. She and Gerda both hated Himmler. Boorman also hushed him when he spoke on the phone or in front of them about the camps. They never believed that the trains were coming simply to deport the Jews, or to re-educate them. What was the point in that?

Gerda had typed the Fuhrer's speech in 1939 that predicted the destruction of the European Jew. Three years later both Alice and Gerda sat by the Fuhrer's side three times in Berlin and once here in the Eagle's Nest, typing speeches that declared the prophecy true. They knew. They all knew, and if they claimed they didn't, they were not listening. Hard choices had to be made sometimes. She had reminded herself of this when she listened and typed.

She closed her eyes. His voice so confident, so sure of his truth, echoed in her mind. "…The result will be not the victory of Jewry, but the annihilation of the Jewish people in Europe."

"My Fuhrer, might I suggest?"

He smiled at Alice and waited. She had been shy about making suggestions, but he was clearly waiting for him.

"Say race, Annihilation of the Jewish race."

The Fuhrer nodded and she made the change. She knew.

Alice watched the sun, so little of it remained on the Horizon. Night was here.

# CHAPTER
# TWENTY-FOUR

THEY WERE DEEP ENOUGH in the woods that there was darkness at ground level long before the sky turned dark. The tree cover could fool you at moments to think it was night, and then a ray of dying light would shine through. Noah was curious if they were safe to let Reiter out and allow him to walk for himself. They were struggling. Marion was the first to crack.

"My left shoulder will never be the same again."

No one responded. They were all tired and in pain. Marion waited for someone, anyone else to complain much longer than she felt she needed to. Noah had a feeling she wanted a break long ago, but he pushed them all further. Being the only woman on this duty, she wanted desperately not to be the first to crumble. Noah could have helped her, but the truth is he wanted to keep moving.

"Can we break? Please."

Mallory responded by stopping. Herzog watched his feet and stopped instantly. They lowered the casket and set it down with a thump. She wrenched her shoulder around.

"There goes your pitching career," Noah quipped.

"The Yankees won't be calling any of us after tonight."

No one else was following their American humor. Noah carried a headlamp but choose to adjust his eyes to the dark. Anke didn't stop, she kept walking. She had no reason to be tried like the rest of them. They all stretched and shook out their shoulders. Noah walked a bit and looked up. There was a faint glow above them in the sky. That was the light of the Eagle's Nest. They were close.

"Can you see anything?" Mallory asked when Noah walked back.

Noah kept his eyes up. "We have a ways to go."

Herzog still weighed down by the heavy ropes sat on a fallen tree. "You think it is dark enough for him to walk his damn self?"

"Still a bit of sun," Noah pointed at the coffin. "We need to be careful."

"Bloody hell," Mallory was not ready. Marion spit before getting low enough to lift her edge. Herzog jumped up to get into position.

Anke came back down the trail. "Almost there."

"Almost where?" Noah asked.

"The place where we need to start climbing."

"Shit," Marion cursed softly.

The four of them lifted the coffin in the air and positioned it awkwardly back onto their shoulders. They moved together faster with the practice. The sky grew purple as they marched, and the light faded like a dying flame. Noah heard a scratch first, it was behind his head but close. He stopped; they all froze. Another scratch, three fingernails dragged along the inside of the coffin. Mallory turned back to look at Noah, his eyes wide. The weight shifted, for the first time, there was movement inside the coffin. They all wanted to drop it like it was on fire, but they couldn't. More scratching, it grew more intense as they carefully lowered the coffin.

"I think it is safe to say night is upon us," Marion said softly.

"Shit," Mallory whispered. "Herzog give me your Hammer."

Herzog pulled out a hammer and spun it around to offer the handle to Mallory.

Anke had stopped on the trail. "What's in the crate?"

"Exactly what it says on the outside," Mallory added as he leaned over the coffin.

"I don't have an Uncle Hans." Anke was not in any mood to hear any more stories. Noah hoped he could distract her, get her away. They could claim Reiter was supposed to meet them here. They couldn't even explain that he was in the coffin, as it was sealed without air holes.

"Anke, could I speak with you in private?" Noah pointed away from the group.

She didn't respond. She didn't trust him. The feeling was mutual. Mallory looked back at Noah; the scratching increased. Reiter was desperate to get out. Maybe now he needed air. Noah had no idea how it worked for his kind.

"I'll go," Mallory stood up. Anke shook her head. She pointed at Noah.

"I will speak to him."

Mallory gave him the 'Don't do it' eyes. Noah sighed and pointed to a clearing closer to the rock bluff. It took only a few seconds before they crossed to the opening at the base of the rock face. Noah looked straight up and could see a soft glow lighting the night. It was the Nest lit like the top of a match. He knew they were lighting torches along the runway. Already they were preparing to escape. The race was still on. Looking up it looked harder to climb than he imagined. One impossible task at a time.

"Noah Samvovich," she said it like a curse.

Noah brought his gaze back down to see Anke pointing her pistol at him. "I thought you were on our side."

"I have no love for the Nazis. Hitler is an evil man, as bad for Germany as he was for the rest of the world."

"Good, this mission is…"

"I think you are just as bad Noah."

Noah laughed. "As Hitler? As bad as your Fuhrer."

She nodded. "Nakam, I know what it means in your language."

"Just a word."

Anke shook her head. "You forget how close I am to power. I have drank Himmler under the table and he talks. About you."

"I hope it was all bad,"

"Himmler knew that word too."

Noah grinned. "I thought we agreed he should feel it."

Anke nodded. "He deserves your vengeance, I agree. We both know Nakam is more than a word."

He knew what she was talking about. He was surprised the Nazis knew. Someone under the promise of survival or escape from the camps had told them. Nation for a nation. Nakam was the Hebrew word for revenge. Also, the code name for a mission that had operatives across Europe, Turkey, and Palestine. He had no reason to lie.

"Nothing was planned until after the war."

"Bullshit, you planned to poison every man, woman, and child in Nuremberg."

Her intelligence was surprisingly good. It wasn't true. He was never involved in such a mission. He knew that freed prisoners had traveled to Palestine to look for poison. He didn't care if she was wrong, he wasn't going to explain to her anything. He had one point burning up from his heart that he couldn't hold back.

"How many dead or tortured Jewish men, women, and children have the people of Nuremberg turned a blind eye to. How many Anke?"

She didn't respond. How could she? She played the role of SS officer. She had blood on those hands. They both knew it.

"The bombs came to Nuremberg my dear, I did nothing to the men, women, and children of that city many of whom evacuated to safety."

She held the gun tightly in his direction. She wasn't lowering it. He could see now that she couldn't come up the mountain with them.

———

Mallory watched Anke and Noah disappear into the trees. As soon as they were out of sight, he turned the hammer towards the coffin. Marion stepped back, she reached into her bag and pulled out the large silver cross that the bishop had blessed for her father. He had dropped it just seconds before he died. Marion's heart raced faster knowing in moments Reiter would be free.

Mallory spun the hammer and dug at the nails. He grunted using all his weight for leverage and pulled the first nail out. Inside the coffin, Reiter scratched more and more desperately. He wished Marion had listened closely when her father lectured her about the biology, the strengths, and weaknesses of the vampire. Even though she lied about knowing her Father's research, he had told her they breathed through the blood, they didn't need air, that they could hunt in high elevations where the oxygen was thin. Mallory had pressed her but they were only wise tales of academics who lived in the pages of books covered in dust to her.

Herzog stepped back. He had witnessed Reiter's power. Maybe if Noah had seen the power of the creature he would have feared him as they did. Mallory popped the first nail and the lid lifted a bit. Reiter's pale hand pushed at the wood. Mallory worked the second nail.

Marion held up the cross. "Don't work too fast Greg."

Mallory popped the second nail and the lid broke off the box. It collapsed and Reiter rolled out onto the German soil for the first time. The creature rolled onto his back and stared up at the trees around them. Marion relaxed seeing him. Rebirth was costly for the vampire; he was not the strong confident-looking man that they saw behind bars that morning.

He looked weak, rotted as a corpse left for months in the grave unattended. She lowered the cross and he turned to her. His four sharp teeth were visible in the faint light.

Mallory stepped back. "He's hungry."

Reiter tried to turn over, it was a great struggle for him to stand. The bones were unnaturally close under the surface of his skin as he stared at Marion. He looked weak now, but when the blood called and the prey was close, the strength would come straight from hell.

She raised the cross. He hissed and looked away.

"Yeah, I believe asshole."

Reiter didn't look at her. His eyes stayed down. "I need blood."

Marion and Mallory shared a look.

"We should've thought of that," whispered Marion.

Reiter turned slowly and looked directly at Mallory. The Brit nodded and looked in the direction where Anke and Noah had disappeared. Mallory sighed deeply; he knew what must happen. Marion felt pain in the pit of her stomach, she couldn't stand the thought of it.

---

Anke was angry. "You have no intention to allow our people a day in court."

Noah didn't want to lie; he shook his head. "I don't."

"You think you have a right to decide who deserves judgment."

"I do."

"The crate has some weapon, some awful thing you plan to unleash on people."

Anke extended her arm to point the pistol almost to his chest. Noah stepped carefully away from her. She took a step closer keeping the gun on him. He could've argued with her. Reminded her what the Nazis had done to his people. It started with the Ghettos, the deportations, the hiding, the constant fear, the starvation, the torture, the experiments, and the agony of watching our loved ones suffer day after day. Skeletons that were barely human, were forced to build the bombs when they didn't have the strength to lift the rotten bread that was just enough to keep the torture going. It ended with mass graves so deep and crowded it could take a hundred years before the bodies are identified.

*Yeah, he had a weapon for them.*

He walked in a circle; eyes locked with her. He watched the barrel of the gun. She followed him exactly as he wished. She turned her back to the direction they came from. He stared at the swastika on her arm. She worked with them; Mallory trusted her but she had also earned Himmler's trust. Noah couldn't ignore that.

In the shadows, he saw the weak form of Count Reiter. He had aged in weeks in death since they sealed him into the coffin this morning. He moved slowly through the darkness towards Anke.

Noah smiled. "I can't forgive, I can't forget."

Anke nodded. She used her thumb to flick the safety off on the pistol. "Then I have no choice."

Reiter attacked; strength came to him as he neared the prey. It was hard to see in the darkness but Noah saw a flash of wings under his arms as he engulfed her. Noah didn't know if it was magic or in his mind. Anke screamed but Reiter put his hand over her mouth. His teeth plunged with force into her neck. She screamed harder with more desperation into the hand.

Noah watched his desiccated hand pumping again with blood. His taut skin gained weight and color instantly as Anke drained like a broken water balloon. Reiter grabbed her head and twisted separating her head from her spine before she could turn. He dropped her body with a thunderous thud.

He wiped the blood away from his mouth. It was strange watching life come back to his body even in the faint light. The unnatural work of resurrection fought with his mind. A good reminder to get used to the impossible, they would see a lot of it before the sun rose again. Over Reiter's shoulder, the rest of the team walked closer. Mallory stood behind him and leaned a bit to see Anke's body.

"Shit," Mallory couldn't look at the grotesque pile for long.

"I'm sorry Greg."

He nodded. "I had a feeling."

Reiter looked up. "She had already betrayed us; we don't have time to waste."

# CHAPTER
# TWENTY-FIVE

ALICE WAS SUPPOSED to get some rest. Heinrich was out at the airstrip making plans and getting the logistics of the landing prepared. Each plane could only carry thirty passengers, but that was as large as they dared to land on the strip. Each passenger's manifest had to be prepared, the passengers had to be ready for boarding and turnaround. If they were going to leave before Dawn.

The landing, loading, and take-off were supposed to happen all in twenty minutes. They had no fuel; they were going to have to re-fuel in Romania. The next plane would have to circle if they took too long. They would have to do it six times between midnight and dawn, to get everyone out. Thanks to the selfless leadership of Heinrich, who might as well be her husband now, they would be on the last plane. He told her to go on an earlier flight but she refused to separate from him until they were safely in the new Fatherland.

It was hard enough for her to let him go do the planning. A part of her worried that his wife and family would appear on the mountain. He didn't mention them, and she wasn't going to. They hadn't been in the bunker with him for months. She was in love with him; they were having a son and his first family was likely dead. It wasn't something she was happy about, but if the rumors were true his wife was probably being tortured by the Russians. His two daughters were likely already in one of Stalin's schools. It was impossible to know.

She lifted the covers of the bed and grabbed her clothes. She couldn't sleep. She was thirsty, hungry, and restless. She knew where the kitchen was. Heidi the house manager, who lived on-site for years, loved visits from her and Gerda. They used to bake cookies with her and dish stories about Berlin. Her husband died in the last war, and she was devout to the Fuhrer.

Alice walked through the halls. The lights were dim in the main room. She looked at her and Gerda's chairs. Two SS officers sat and watched the moonlit peaks. They were speaking in hushed tones, there had been joy upon making it to the Nest, a feeling of escape but the daunting nature of the rest of the night had sunk in.

The kitchen light was on. Alice slowly opened the door and found the kitchen trashed. Opened cans, packages, and dirty plates piled in the sink. Krista Hausser, a middle-aged woman still in her SS uniform, unbuttoned and out of regulations, leaned near the sink smoking. She was not that old but Alice had seen her picture before and she looked like she had aged decades in the last two years. She smiled and pointed to the dishes in the sink.

"Leave it for the Russians."

Alice laughed. She didn't have the energy to correct her that the South was facing the advancement of the Americans. Krista had a sweet smile, even at this dark moment it was comforting. She waved Alice closer and they shared a hug. Alice didn't know she was holding anything in until she began weeping into Krista's shoulder. She gave soft pets to Alice's head with the lit cigarette still between her fingers.

"It's alright my dear, it's alright."

Alice remained in the hug for a long moment until she felt some strength return. It felt as if she were in her mother's arms, with her eyes closed she forgot the war.

Alice pulled out of the hug. "Thank you."

"We could all use a hug right now."

Alice smiled at that. She went to the fridge and looked for milk but there was none left. She grabbed a glass and let the water run in the faucet for five seconds as Heidi taught her before filling her glass. The water was cold, it didn't have far to travel from the well.

Krista pushed her a package of cookies. Half of the dozen were already eaten. She had never met this woman but she knew who she was. Alice had typed letters to her from The Fuhrer, including letters about the sacrifice of her son who died in the battle of Stalingrad. She managed the embassy of the occupation authority in Paris. She worked directly under both Otto and C.H. von Stülpnagel. She'd stayed in France throughout the war and had a reputation as the mother of Paris. She cared for officers and infantry like they were her own boys. A shoulder to cry on, known for her compassion for the common soldier. The carrot and the stick. She had been the carrot and Otto the stick.

Otto had ordered the first executions of Jews and Communists in France. Alice wasn't sure about her role but remembered the letter she typed to her. The Fuhrer thanked her for her loyalty, and dedication to making hard choices.

"I'm Alice."

"Krista..."

"I know you. I worked for the Fuhrer." Alice twiddled her fingers to signal that she typed for him. Krista nodded and took her last drag before tossing the cigarette in the sink.

"Were you there in Berlin?"

Alice nodded.

"Poor thing," Krista sighed. "So, it is true that he is dead? Some of these babies in uniform insist that he is still working magic to save the Fatherland."

Alice made a finger gun to her head.

"Bastard."

Alice was shocked. Krista almost laughed. "True believer still, here at the top of the world running like the Communists to bread lines. My dear, it is no time for belief."

"Why are you here if not to still fight?"

"We made lots of bad decisions Alice." Krista looked around nervously. "Where is a good place to get some fresh air?"

"It's cold outside."

Krista grabbed two mugs and poured herself a steaming cup of coffee. "Drink up, we have a long night ahead of us."

Alice took the coffee and pointed to the balcony. They passed an officer who wept quietly in the corner. Many of these men were not just leaving behind their way of life and country but their families. Krista's eyes lingered on the man while Alice grabbed two blankets.

They wrapped themselves in the blankets and stepped outside. They had a view of the airstrip. The lights were lined up but they had added torches all along each side to make it even clearer. The orange glow shined on Krista's face. The wind blew her hair back. The air was bitterly cold but it felt refreshing to stand here.

"Alice, may I ask a question about your relationship with the Fuhrer?"

Alice didn't want to talk about him.

"Did he ever express regret, in private? Away from all the Reich. When you were alone?"

Alice thought about the first time she typed for Hitler. It was hard to think of him as a person at the time. She had seen his pictures, seen him flicker by in news reels. Heard his booming voice on the radio. She had not even seen him speak in 1938 when Martin Boorman hired her. She was struck by how short he was. How soft-spoken away from the attention.

"I'm not sure." Alice shrugged. "Maybe to Eva, I don't remember."

Krista nodded. "I am not surprised."

Alice wasn't sure what she meant. She didn't like the sound of it. It sounded disloyal. Here they were trying against all hope to keep the dream of the thousand-year Reich alive. What was she saying? Krista was watching her face. With the blanket covering her uniform she looked like just another German mother.

"He did this to us, his hubris."

Alice wanted to tell her to stop. To remind her that she made choices. All of Germany made choices. Before she could speak, she heard something. A bell rang. It was from the far guard tower. The soldiers ran shouting. "Alert! Alert!"   Others screamed inside the house. "Lights out! Lights out!"

The soldiers working the airstrip threw water from buckets on the torches. The lights along the strip flickered and disappeared. Behind them, one by one the lights in the manor went out. They could see officers running to make sure the many house lights went dark. Moment to moment, the darkness grew, the only light was from the moon.

"No one could've followed us!" Alice pleaded. "They mined the road."

Krista pushed her to the floor of the balcony, she shushed her even as the officers running in the house continued to make noise. She could hear thunderous footsteps as the last lights went out.

"This is insane, we are safe here!"

Then she heard it. The low far-off hum of plane engines. It was two hours before the Luftwaffe was scheduled to arrive. The sound came from engines too massive to land here. She knew that sound, it had been months since she'd heard it. In the last days before they went into the bunker for good that sound would send them running. American bombers.

"Damn it!" Alice pounded the balcony. "No point in being quiet."

"We don't want them to see us."

Alice peered between the wood planks that decorated the balcony. Mostly invisible until the last moments, they were like birds of prey across the sky. The bombers were half a dozen across, coming from the west in their direction. *They know we're here*, Alice cringed inside. They were moments from dying. They had made it this far, but now they had nowhere left to run. She heard a scream inside the house. The sound of a young child crying was then muffled by a hand. It was irrational, they could not be heard, but terror makes you lose your mind.

The planes grew closer and louder each second.

# CHAPTER
# TWENTY-SIX

NOAH KEPT his eyes on Reiter as they walked slowly up the peak. The pine trees shook in the high mountain breeze. They had to step softly and quietly to make sure they didn't step on any fallen branches. The rest of the group walked behind him. He didn't pay any attention to them. The light from the manor was like a beacon above. The air was cold but they were moving fast enough to stay warm. They had moved mostly in silence. They had only seen the one guard whom Reiter had killed before the rest of them even knew he was there.

This wasn't Noah's first night climb, but it was the highest. He was just as scared as the rest but chose not to show it. Reiter saw right through him the moment he grabbed Noah with his ice-cold hand. Noah instinctively crawled but was relieved to be on solid ground. As much as he enjoyed the relief, the unnaturally cold hand starkly reminded him that Reiter was no man.

By the time they pulled Mallory up over the rock face to the peak, Marion and Herzog had relaxed. Watching Reiter pull them up and dispatch the guard so fast should've inspired fear, but Noah had to keep in mind that for the moment they were on the same side. Now as they walked, Noah felt like he must keep his eyes on him, even if it was futile.

"Hey can we take a little break," Marion whispered behind him. Noah turned to see her struggling. The air was thin, and the grade of the hill intense. Reiter shook his head but found a stump. They were still a fifteen-minute walk from the building.

"There are no guards nearby."

Reiter could smell them better than a bloodhound so they all relaxed. Noah put up five fingers. He didn't like stopping but he couldn't risk wearing out the team. Noah found a grassy spot and sat down. Mallory reached into his pack and pulled out a container of rations. He tore open the condensed meatloaf and ate it with his fingers.

"How can you be hungry at a time like this?"

Herzog shushed her.

Reiter turned around and they all jumped. "Relax and speak freely. We are alone."

Marion almost laughed. "So comforting."

The vampire stood over Noah, he looked up at the creature. He felt sweat form on the small of his back. This close he could see the teeth as he attempted to smile. It was an uncomfortable feeling. The creature lowered himself down. Marion rose with her cross, Reiter gave her an angry stare.

"May I sit with my compatriot?"

Noah pointed to the ground.

Reiter sat next to him.

"Do you get tired?" Herzog asked.

Reiter laughed. "Not like you, but it is best to conserve my energy. If you want to wait here…"

"We're on this mission too." Noah knew Reiter thought they were all unnecessary.

"They have to invite you in you know," Marion seemed to think that was a gotcha.

"Not everything your father taught you is true."

"But that one is true," Noah pointed at him.

"The human mind is very suggestible."

Mallory chewed on his food and stared at Reiter. Noah knew he was still having messy feelings about what the creature did to Anke. Time to change the subject.

"We need to get a closer look at the manor before we..."

"I know the exact layout."

Noah shook his head. "We know nothing about the interior of the Nest."

"The guard?" Marion asked.

Reiter nodded.

"The one I saw fall off the mountain?" Asked Mallory.

"The Count here," Marion pointed at him. "He doesn't just consume blood."

"Souls?" Mallory asked.

"I'm surprised the Germans have any." Noah quipped.

"And their knowledge hits me like a flash but it is here." Reiter pointed to his skull. He turned to Mallory. "She didn't love you... Anke."

"I know who you meant, I never thought she did."

"She thought you were an honorable man and thought Noah was a murderer."

Noah ignored that. They all saw her pull the weapon on him. He could live with the judgment of a woman who was still ultimately a Nazi. He looked up at the light of the Nest. There it was. That opulent manor was home right now to the worst killers in history. He was finally here ready to unleash evil unto evil. Excitement was an understatement, and satisfaction filled him. He could put up with any of it as long as he was able to make the bastards pay.

They sat in the silence of the mountain for several minutes. Noah was about to suggest that they start moving when he heard it. It was far off still, but the buzz was like nothing else. B-17 bombers. He knew they had no orders to bomb this place but it wasn't beyond Eisenhower or Patrick to change their minds. His mission to recover the plans for German atomic weapons was the only reason the brass had agreed to this mission.

*What if they decided it was unlikely that their atomic plans remained on the mountain? What if they decided that they were expendable?*

Noah looked at Mallory. "You hear that?"

Mallory nodded. "Getting closer. You don't think they changed their minds at central command?"

"If they did, it was nice knowing you all."

"Shit," Marion closed her eyes. They turned back to the Eagle's Nest. They were shouting in German, turning out lights as fast as they could. The Nazi terror amused Noah but he didn't want them to die that quickly. Reiter watched the Nest and enjoyed the fear and chaos that you didn't need to be a vampire to sense.

Herzog stood up and grabbed Mallory's binoculars out of his bag. He went to a clearing and looked. They would be invisible in the darkness still. They roared closer and crossed the spotlight of the moon's glow. Herzog cursed in German. "B-17's coming east straight for us, five, maybe more."

Marion pulled on his arm; it hadn't occurred to him that they might survive the shelling of the mountain.

"Noah, goddamn it!"

Noah waved them behind a large rock outcropping and from there they could see the massive planes swooping in like hawks on a rat. They could feel the disturbance in the air, it was as if the mechanical beasts were tearing apart the mountains' peace and tranquility by hand.

"Keep going you sons of bitches," Noah screamed.

"Bloody bastards," Mallory said only loud enough that Noah heard them over the propellor roar.

Noah closed his eyes and did as he had a dozen times since they crossed the border, a thousand times since he left home in Minneapolis and joined this war. He prayed to God to let him live and finish this mission. He started with the Shema. Shouting over the roar in Hebrew.

"Hear O Israel, grant me this night!"

# CHAPTER
# TWENTY-SEVEN

THE ROAR of the planes seemed to consume the night whole. Alice wished for the strength to pull the bombers from the sky. Krista covered her ears and buried her face in the blanket. Alice chose to face the monster she stared at one plane in the formation that was closest to them. They had terrified the village already and now the plane flew over so close Alice was sure she saw bolts in its underbelly. Everything shook, the power of six planes each with four large propellors was nothing short of an earthquake as they went over.

The building shook but a few moments later the sound and shaking faded. Alice jumped up and ran to the front of the house. The officers in the room were emerging from under tables. She stopped at the front door, she wouldn't open it Through the windows beside the front door, she saw the bombers fade into the east. Cheers went up around the building before the lights came back on.

Alice took deep breaths. Heinrich appeared in front of the house he was giving orders to re-light the airstrip. Krista walked up behind her. "Maybe we will survive this."

Alice sighed. "I left my coffee out on the balcony."

———

The mountain shook for thirty seconds or as many years. It was torture for those moments. The plane was so low over the mountain, the power in the air so intense it could've been a bomb. Noah held his eyes closed and prayed in his mind. It was easy to picture his own death at that moment. It was a thought he'd had so many times throughout this war. This was it, the end.

Searching his heart for a prayer it went to his Bar Mitzvah, standing at the Torah, his eyes from time to time finding his parents in the front row. He hated Hebrew school; his mother insisted. His father was content to take him fishing in the summer with his friends from work and their boys. His mother told him many times that he would understand one day. You are meant to understand during your Bar Mitzvah. That is what means to become a grown Jewish man.

He didn't like being Jewish then. He was the only Jew on the baseball team. He was tall for his age and a good player. They called him Four-Eyes and the Jew Moose before he started getting hits. Then he was just Moose or Sammy-Moose. When you are a little boy, you don't want to be different. They lived two blocks south of the line that would've sent him to Lincoln with the other Jewish boys. He was alone at Jefferson; he didn't like his name which gave him away and always got changed to Sandwich by the gang clowning around. He felt that way all through boot and even when he first came to Europe.

He never felt bad about it until the first time he met a family hiding from the Nazis. With each inhumanity, the Reich put on his people he thought back to that boy. That boy who hated being Jewish, who learned the Torah just to keep his mother from skinning him. He didn't want to learn Hebrew then, he just wanted the party and presents. That boy didn't become a man that day and now here under the raging roar of American bombers afraid to die. He whispered the prayer he remembered best from that day.

"Blessed are You, Lord our God, King of the universe, who has chosen us from among all the nations and given us His Torah. Blessed…"

The roar faded second to second. He let his heart slow a bit before opening his eyes. He stared at the moon, easy to mistake it as full, but it had two nights to go before that. It was so close it felt within reach. There was quiet again. He whispered but, in the silence, it felt like a savage scream.

"...are You, Lord, who gives the Torah."

They were still alive. The mission was still on and Mallory heard the end of his prayer. "Mazel Tov," he whispered.

Noah laughed. "Indeed."

Noah looked up over the rock. Reiter never hid, never left the path, he just stared up at the Eagle's Nest still hiding in Darkness.

Mallory stood on the rock and watched the bombers disappear into the vast night. He turned to look at Noah. "Well, here we are."

Noah nodded. He pushed the image of his proud parents out of his mind, the feeling of the whole synagogue and the community showering him with candy. He fumbled the words that day but Rabbi was proud of him too, a man born here in Europe, who spoke at Sabbath of peace and harmony. He couldn't focus on the happy memories. They were not the fuel he needed. He thought about the family he found in Holland who had starved hiding in an attic. Their only other choice was deportation, and the camps. He chose to see their faces.

Noah unclipped his holster. "No more time to waste."

They followed Reiter to the path. The vampire suddenly ran faster than they could follow. His steps barely touched the ground. Noah refused to drop his pack but took off after him. The speed was incredible, the only thing more amazing was the silence with which he moved.

Noah ran as fast as he could, not thinking about where until suddenly he emerged from the tree line and had to stop. He was visible in the glowing light of the torches along the airstrip. The only thing that saved him was the fact that the German guard was staring off in the opposite direction, towards where the plane had disappeared.

He dropped back before he was seen and had to push Mallory back. He held his hand over his mouth. When they turned around and looked from their hiding position Reiter was already gone. Noah held up a finger to signal for them all to wait. They were probably thirty or forty feet from the back of a German guard who stood just under a large balcony. They were goddamn lucky not to have been seen.

Either way, the assault had begun.

# CHAPTER
# TWENTY-EIGHT

<u>May 1<sup>st</sup> 10:28 PM: Eagle's Nest</u>

ALICE OPENED the door that led to the balcony just as Krista stepped inside. The woman gave her a disarming smile. They had survived a frightening moment together. She reminded Alice of her mother and wished for a moment she could see her, just to say goodbye. It had been months since her last update on her parents. She may never see them again and she just had to accept that. Maybe Krista could fill that void. Krista must've sensed her feelings, she rubbed her shoulder.

"Better get inside my dear, we will be leaving soon."

Alice held up a finger. "I left my coffee outside; I'll be just a moment."

The brisk mountain air hit a little harder than she expected, having dropped the blanket along the way. She'd left the mug sitting on the edge of the balcony before they saw the planes. She saw the ring it left on the wood but the cup was gone. It must have fallen off when the planes flew over and shook the entire mountain. Alice leaned over and saw the white mug lying in the grass.

It was only a few feet behind the guard staring up at the sky where the planes had disappeared. He was an enlisted man in the army like her Heinrich. He could easily throw her the mug.

"Excuse me."

She realized how silly it was. They were leaving behind trucks; Heidi wasn't around to count plates and bowls. It didn't matter if she left a mug, but it was in her nature to clean up after herself. The soldier turned around and looked up at her.

"Yes, fraulein?"

"Never mind. It's silly."

He was a young man, barely old enough looking for the war. He wouldn't have been a few years ago, but after a few pushes into Russian fronts, he was. He smiled at her as he stepped closer to the balcony. His boot kicked the mug and he didn't even notice it. "No, what is it?"

"My coffee mug," she pointed to his feet. "I dropped it."

He slung his rifle over his shoulder and smiled. "You want it back?"

Alice shrugged. The soldier leaned over to grab the mug. That is when the darkness moved. Alice thought her eyes were playing tricks. The night came together and grabbed the soldier. It happened so fast she saw only a blur. He rose off his feet and was pulled back into the woods.

Alice leaned over the balcony and only her mug remained. She scanned the woods wanting to call his name but realized she'd never asked for it. Then two twitching legs, she saw them for an instant and they slid back into the woods. She screamed. She didn't want to, her body did it for her. Across the airstrip, Heinrich and several of the enlisted men were preparing for the flights.

They ran closer to her position. Krista and several of the SS officers came out onto the balcony. Krista pulled her into a hug, now there were men on the ground and all around staring at her.

"What happened?" Heinrich yelled from below. Krista squared her shoulders and looked her in the eyes.

"Alice?"

Alice pulled away and looked into the woods. "Something took the guard."

Heinrich and his men looked at each other. "There was a guard on patrol right there and something took him."

"Otto?" Heinrich asked.

One of the soldiers nodded. Heinrich signaled them to go into the woods. Four of the men lifted their rifles and went into the woods. She relaxed some knowing they were looking. The door to the Balcony was still open. Himmler stepped out. Einhard Goring who had been such trouble on the truck was sweaty drunk. He half-heartedly saluted Himmler, who ignored him.

"What is it?" Himmler looked straight at Alice.

Goring spoke as if he was the one Himmler addressed. "It is nothing sir, hysterical woman."

Alice hated to give the drunk oaf any credit but she was unsure of herself. "He was there, and then he was gone."

Goring laughed, and several of the officers laughed with him. She knew she saw something. Himmler joined in the laughter. He grabbed her hand he thought it would be comforting. His hand was moist and sweaty, his handkerchief was rough, stuffed back in his uniform pocket. "My dear nothing can make it up here. We are safe."

The Fuhrer didn't trust this man in the final days. Now as he tried to assure her, she heard the Fuhrer's voice cursing this man. She looked into the eyes behind the thin wire-rimmed glasses. She wanted to ask them *Why the guards then? Why had they raced to turn out the lights before planes flew over?* His eyes. She looked for fear, she saw nothing. He didn't understand.

"Something is out there," Alice didn't like how shaky her voice sounded. "What was the soldier's name?"

Himmler shrugged. Of course, he didn't know.

"Otto," Krista said meekly. "They said his name was Otto."

Alice nodded. "Something took Otto."

Himmler stepped closer. She smelled the cigar and Schnapps on his breath. "This journey to the new Fatherland is dangerous enough, we don't need hysteria."

With that Himmler turned and walked back into the building. Goring like a puppy followed after giving the women an amused look. One by one the officers followed Himmler. Only

Krista remained with her. The sweet motherly-looking woman rubbed her shoulder. "What did you see really?"

Alice felt an ice-cold chill go through her whole body trying to visualize it. She couldn't think of anything else. "Darkness, pure darkness."

Krista nodded. She didn't seem surprised. Her eyes spoke of fear.

"You believe me?"

Krista nodded. "Here? What else could it be?"

# CHAPTER
# TWENTY-NINE

May 1st 10:48 PM: Eagle's Nest

ALICE LOOKED out the window and listened to the conversation going on behind her. Little had changed. The Fuhrer would often sit at the small bar at the end of the living room and have loud conversations both important and trivial. He and his men would often ignore or forget her and Gerda sitting there. They heard plenty of things they were not supposed to. She could watch them reflected in the window.

Goring was almost drunk enough to forget that they were on the losing end of a war. The SS officers were safe and warm inside drinking while the German army soldiers were outside doing the work of preparing for escape. Goring had drunk most of his liquor with Wolfgang Schmitt. He was an early party member who worked under Himmler doing deportations and eventually became an administrator during the Polish occupation. He'd vacationed here with the Fuhrer once just before the war. Alice had typed letters to him several times.

"Perhaps it is for the better in the end." Goring had no idea how loud his voice was as he sat on the stool by the small bar. Schmitt kept looking at his empty glass but wouldn't think to pour his own drink.

"How the fuck is this better?" said Schmitt.

Himmler sat in a chair nursing a Schnapps that hadn't been sipped since before they all ran outside. He and his second in command Wilhelm Frick seemed amused by the conversation.

"Adolf was holding us back." Goring reached for a bottle across the bar. He sat back when he couldn't reach it. He laughed a bit when he hit the chair.

"Don't talk of the Fuhrer that way," Schmitt lost his sense of humor quickly. "Not tonight."

"The Reich was never about him," Himmler took a sip. Frick nodded. "Mister Goring is drunk but the point is one we must consider. It is obvious the trap we fell into."

Frick nodded. "The Jews lured him, what better way to destroy Europe than to exploit the sympathy of the entire world. The only way the Jews could do that is to play victim."

"The Communist scum, the filthy perverts and mongrel half-breed gypsies," Himmler nodded. "Europe was already a cesspool. We tried to save it and now the destruction is complete, our sacred Aryan lands will become a northern Zion."

Frick held up his drink. "We live to build a new stronger Fatherland and one day we will return."

Goring lifted his empty glass.

Alice stood up. Schmitt watched her. She walked to the front window and looked outside. The guards that Heinrich sent out had not returned. She looked at the clock above the bar. More than ten minutes had passed. Plenty of time for a sweep of the grounds. Alice walked over to Himmler.

"Excuse me Reichfuhrer."

Himmler turned to her and he was surprised she was still there despite never leaving the room. He sat his glass down on a table.

"Fuhrer," said Frick.

Alice was confused, her eyes danced between the two stoic men.

"My title has changed my dear." Himmler's expression didn't change. How quickly they were willing to throw dirt on the man who gave them everything.

"I meant no disrespect; I was under the impression that Goebbels was chancellor now."

"Briefly," Himmler spoke flatly. "But he chose to stay with his Fuhrer beyond the end."

Goring put his fingers like a gun to his temple as if she was too stupid to understand what Himmler was telling her. She hated the idea of this. The Fuhrer didn't trust Himmler and now here she was following him to the other side of the world and he was demanding the respect of the title she never thought would be given to another.

"Fuhrer." It was hard not to wrap the word in venom. "The guards have not returned."

They laughed. All four of the SS officers laughed at her. She waited until they were done.

"The guards went to search ten minutes ago and have not returned. I am telling you that something is out there."

Frick sighed deeply. He was annoyed. She didn't care. Himmler's eyes seemed to scan her. He started at her feet and slowly went up her body to her eyes.

"You worked for him, didn't you?"

Alice nodded. "Typing letters mostly."

"I remember you," Himmler spoke softly. "Why are you here?"

Alice felt the floor come out under her. He did nothing to hide the meaning of his question. She was a loyal German, loyal to the party, to the Fuhrer right to the end. She should not have to explain herself. She shouldn't have to be where she was.

"Heinrich Hitzinger," she pointed in the direction where he was outside. She put her hand on her belly. "We are having a son."

"Ahh yes the Sergeant," Himmler smiled because he was supposed to. "You know it is a boy?"

Alice nodded. "I can feel him. Fount of life, Germany needs pure sons. His father is…"

"He is a brave warrior. Do you not trust him to protect us?"

She did, but it was hard to explain what she saw. Himmler was annoyed, they all were. She felt it like knives on her skin.

"Go to your room Alice," Goring sounded sober for a

moment. Alice hated to take orders from him, but they were not taking her seriously. She had to find help, someone they would listen to. Alice stormed away. When she was out of sight, she heard the men laugh.

# CHAPTER
# THIRTY

REITER ACCEPTED LONG AGO that his power came to him from the Devil. Strigoi, vampire, or whatever name was given to his condition by the people around the world was proof that the king of darkness existed, and he was its servant. The origin of this affliction was rumored to be such, but no one really knew. Over the years, as knowledge of the cosmos grew, he thought the source might be beyond the heavens in the stars. He could have been transformed by an alien disease. Moment to moment he thought of it as a gift or a curse, but he always returned to it being something magical. He had accepted that he was evil, driven by a hunger that was nearly impossible to feed. The universe or the devil had made him the perfect hunter.

He was born human and still connected by the thinnest of threads to the species. His reflection was that of a man, although it was faint and almost invisible just as the legends warned. One reason he hunted humans so well is he enjoyed living in their memories and dreams. He would gladly sleep forever and savor the lives of souls he consumed. He was never proud of what he had become, a parasite leeching off the world for countless years of undeath. His only escape was to live inside their memories.

This mission was a gift. For the first time in centuries, he felt his humanity stir. He had something good he could do for the world. The Nazis were beyond evil, something deeper and darker. They didn't consume. They destroyed, tortured, controlled, and erased with calm cruelty he found disgusting. Each time he took the life of one he gained their experience, so little conscience. Most had an absolute righteous belief in what they were doing.

He followed the four Nazi soldiers silently through the woods. Floating just above the surface he never stepped on a thing, that would have warned them. They finally stopped wasting their breath asking for him to come out with hands raised. Reiter closed his eyes and followed the beat of their hearts.

He smelled Viktor, in the lead. Sweat pouring from him. Viktor was Otto's friend and a bad boy. Otto was bent over reaching for the mug when Reiter took him. His fear spiked and Reiter learned many things about Otto. During his childhood in Leipzig, his father never returned from the Great War, and his stepfather beat him and insisted that he was his real father. His mother applauded on the street when the Jewish shops were closed, as well as the day he joined Hitler-Jugend. His battles in northern Italy, the one where he lost hearing in his left ear, and his first day on duty at Treblinka. That is where he met his good friend Viktor.

They spent months freezing together in a tower overlooking the camp. There was no forced labor there. It had only one purpose. The train arrived and it was not long before the prisoners were told to board another train but the journey was over. The gas was most effective but a few survived long enough for screams to be heard at night from the graves before they were covered. Sometimes the trains would be empty for days at a time before they covered the graves.

Otto rationalized it but Reiter experienced his fear at hearing the screams when his blood flowed into him. Otto didn't like the screams but it was not what he felt guilty about. Reiter had to dig deep into his mind but hidden away was a secret he kept with Viktor, a secret by the name of Rebecca.

*He and Viktor had duty in the tower at night. The winters were long, and the front was lonely. Viktor was a young man when he left for war. He admitted to Otto that he'd never had a lover, Otto had a girlfriend, back home. He kept a picture of Grace in his pocket always. Many of the officers were lonely, away from their families, and plenty of them did it. It wasn't talked about, but Viktor was there when the trains came in and he watched the arrivals. He looked for women in the crowds of Jews who were rare beauties. To the mentality of these monsters, these women were bound for death, what harm could it be.*

*He saw Rebecca; she had a son and daughter holding each of her hands. She was clean, wearing a dress. Beautiful. For a Jew. Viktor called her away from the line for the last train. She held her children tight. He took her to the small cabin they shared. Otto didn't know what happened behind those doors and Viktor asked him to come back in five minutes. When he returned, Viktor was waiting outside with the children. Otto didn't want to learn their names.*

*"Take them back to the line," Viktor said it  without looking at the children.*

*Otto did look at the children. They were too scared to speak. They would not walk without their mother's hand. He thought it possible they knew they were dying, what they didn't know was that their mother had agreed to let Viktor have his way with her to save their lives. Otto pulled out his pistol and pointed back toward the train with his pistol.*

*"My name is…"*

*"Shut up," Otto didn't want to know. It didn't matter.*

*The boy tried to talk a few more times before the end of the walk. He looked a year older than his sister, he held her hand now as they walked.  They cried with each step away from their mother, the Jews in the line watched them return. One older man asked in German where she was, but Otto ignored them all. One Jewish woman took them into her arms. Otto left as quickly as he could.*

*He returned to his cabin and saw that Viktor had put a belt on the door. There were screams, he tried not to listen, when Viktor came out to get the belt off the door, he was shirtless. He didn't say a word. Otto wanted to get sleep before his duty and went straight to his bed across the room from Viktor.*

*He was in the shower, singing an opera not even close to correct. Otto struggled to get his boot off and heard a sound across the room. He peered down and was shocked.*

*Rebecca, he later learned her name, was chained under the bed. A gag in her mouth. Her face was red from the tears. Otto stared at her for a moment but sat up. He could only see her shoes, they looked like a pair Grace wore. He stared at the shoes until Viktor came out, his clothes fresh, his hair wet. They shared a look, and Viktor whispered to him.* "Her children are alive if she asks."

*Ruthie and Edward. She called out their names during her nightmares. She had many of them before Viktor grew tired of her.*

Reiter had grown tired of Viktor. He rose up over the Nazi and landed in his path. Viktor stopped and lifted his rifle, but he was too stunned to fire or squeeze the trigger. He didn't see Reiter; he saw the glowing form of Rebecca. He saw her in a stunning dress that hung off her shoulders, her hair was curled and bouncing softly on the breeze, he saw lips full and red. Viktor was stunned to silence, the men behind him stopped when he did. They saw a mist forming in the darkness

"*Viktor,*" Reiter spoke in her voice. "*Where are my children?*"

"No, No." He shook his head.

"Sir," One of the soldiers behind spoke and raised his rifle.

"*You said you would save them.*"

Viktor stepped back but Reiter followed matching his steps. He only saw Rebecca, her features turning slowly from beauty to decay.

"No, I killed..."

Reiter put a finger up to stop him. He saw Rebecca's withering hand. "*You did, my body that you used like a toy is rotting in a mass grave, and yet here we are Viktor. Here we are.*"

He turned to look away. He had to escape the sight of her becoming a corpse in front of him. His soldiers were gone. He only saw Otto holding the hands of Ruthie and Edward. Reiter leaned over his shoulder and spoke inside his mind as Rebecca. *They will never leave you unless you kill them now. Kill them Viktor or they will be here in your mind. My sweet Ruthie, my dear Edward. Forever with you...*

Viktor lifted his MG-15 and fired a burst of rounds. The thunderous fire echoed around the quiet night on the mountain and was heard across the Alps. When the bodies hit the ground, they were his soldiers. Viktor turned to face Rebecca. Her face had melted away and he peered past her skin to her skull. Her voice crawled inside his head, exploding louder than thunder. *I will always be here Viktor, always, always, always.*

Viktor dropped the rifle and unholstered his pistol he pointed it at Rebecca's ghostly form. He fired but she disappeared. She was behind him.

*You can't kill me twice. Only one escape, Viktor. You killed your men. You will not be welcome in the new Fatherland and if you are, I will be there.*

Viktor looked at the pistol and knew what he must do. He put it under his chin. Her voice was like a hammer inside his head.

*Do it Viktor.*

He looked at the bodies of his dead men. He heard the sounds of boots coming closer. They'd heard the shots and would see only him as the murderer. Viktor pushed the pistol tighter under his chin. He cried, not wanting to do it, but he also couldn't live like this.

He looked into Rebecca's eyes for the last time and felt the hatred burn like a thousand rockets. She spoke. *Bang.* Viktor squeezed the trigger and in his last second alive he saw Reiter's smiling face.

# CHAPTER
# THIRTY-ONE

THE HALLS of the manor were dark. Only a few faint lights flickered in the halls. Most of the officers were following the orders to get rest. Himmler had promised to notify their families later. She wondered how many believed him. More than once, she heard weeping even through the doors as she made her way to the third floor. She had stayed many times there; she didn't ask for her old room in the chaos but Krista was in a room three doors down from Gerda's old room. Being up here brought a flood of memories of better times. She stopped and put her hand on the door that had been hers.

Inside she heard Irma, the mother from the truck yelling at her son. "Let me rest, please lay down!"

This startled Alice, feeling the need for some comfort, she moved on to the room where Krista was staying. She knocked on her door. No response. Alice saw the light under the door. Movement.

"Please Krista, I need to talk."

The door opened, the sweet motherly woman stood in the doorway wiping away tears. Krista put her finger over her mouth. They were surrounded by rooms with sleeping officers.

"Quiet," she whispered. "Some of them are sleeping believe it or not."

"They don't believe me. Himmler, Goring, they mocked me." Alice whispered. "Can I come in?"

Krista didn't budge. "I want to be alone sweetheart."

Something had changed in her. The scare with the planes. Her strength and compassion had melted away. Dark circles had formed under her eyes in the last few minutes.

"I think you could use the chat too Krista."

Krista looked down the hall and then back at her. "You said the darkness took him."

"I'm not sure what I saw."

"We are not so close to heaven that he can't find us." Her voice quivered; she was afraid to even speak the words.

"Who are you talking about?"

Krista looked away from Alice and held on to the cross around her neck. "My father was a priest you know. I didn't think my duty to the state was a contradiction. I was proud when the Fuhrer sent me to France. I believed God had chosen him."

"He was chosen."

Krista nodded. "I thought so, I believed it. I gave my son to the war, his body is scattered on Russian soil, we had nothing of Martin to bury."

"He died for the…"

"The glory of the Reich. Is this the glory?"

"Don't disrespect his sacrifice, Krista."

"You want to lecture me? I gave up my son, and worse."

"What could be worse?"

"I was a good mother, Martin was loved," Krista shook. "I ordered the Communists and anarchists arrested. Some fled Spain when we helped Franco, many were just students, little more than children. Their Mamas and Papas sent them to university. I ordered them taken away. I knew they would be killed. I cleared Paris of radicals and Jews. We were not blind to what was happening to them."

"No, no Krista they are not like us." Alice pleaded. "They're cancer. You know this, Europe would never recover if…"

"That," Krista pointed at her. "...is why the darkness is coming for us."

In the distance, machine gun fire echoed across the Alps.

Krista grinned "They think they can kill what is coming."

Shouts and orders followed outside. Doors opened around the building. No one missed the sound. Before they arrived, they were all told they were safe and just had to wait. That no one could hurt them. No one could stop them.

"What the hell is happening?" One of the officers hastily tied a robe. The officers staying on this floor had all stepped out and stared at each other confused. Alice didn't know their names but she knew the type. Early party faithful that had helped the Fuhrer rise to power. Now they avoided the most dangerous aspects of war. Part of units, long ago disbanded, that the Fuhrer continued to order about.

You could hear boots pounding across the halls in every direction. The enlisted soldiers outside shouted commands. Chaos had broken out. Another single shot echoed out into the night.

Krista leaned closer to Alice. "You asked what's worse than losing a child. I did the same damn thing to so many mothers. I lost my boy and my soul." She fought tears. "I need to make peace with God, you should do the same."

The door slammed in Alice's face. Alice looked at the door. She turned to see the SS officers, mostly in robes staring at her. She listened to the screams and chaos. She felt the fear and confusion of the men in the hall. They didn't know what to do. She dropped her hand to her belly. Her son was not developed enough to make his presence known. She just wanted to live to see Heinrich and the boy play

# CHAPTER
# THIRTY-TWO

<u>May 1<sup>st</sup> 10:58 PM: Eagle's Nest</u>

ONCE NOAH WAS on the north side of the building, he relaxed a bit. That was until he saw how close the back of the building was to the edge and drop-off. He didn't see any guards, because why would they guard such a ledge. He could follow the low hum of the generator. The only path was the ledge behind the building or going all the way around.

Noah walked carefully as there was not much room for feet, the drop-off felt to him like hundreds of feet. It was impossible to know because he saw only mist. He heard the sounds of glasses clinking and loud drunken talk. The walls muffled it so he didn't know what they were saying.

He was surprised and a little disappointed that they would be so merry after losing the war. He had to believe that it would make what was coming so much sweeter. The light from the large window was enough for him to see the ledge. He took a deep breath and put his back on the wall. He walked sideways across it faster than he should have.

Noah crossed over to a space with more ground to stand on and took in a lungful of diesel fumes coming off the generator.

It felt better to have room to stand, but he didn't have time to waste. Still, ten feet away he saw the large steel fuel tanks, the wiring that led to the building, and the guard. Noah almost cursed. The guard sat sleeping in a chair beside the machine.

He wasn't worried about being heard, the generator was not loud but enough to mask his approach. The guard had on a helmet and trench coat. His rifle was propped up by his chair. This would be a dilemma for some. He was asleep and helpless. During his first year in the war when he was still wearing the army uniform, he might have paused, may have just given him a bump and knocked him out. That Noah, who had just left Minnesota, had never seen or smelled a Nazi death camp.

The smell was on his mind as he pulled out his knife. He stepped behind the guard and positioned the knife inches from the back of his neck.

Machine gun fire echoed around the mountain. It was loud enough to be heard over the hum of the generator. The guard was startled awake. He reached for his rifle but never got it. In one motion Noah pushed the knife into his neck, he squeezed the handle tight and gave it a little push. The knife broke through, and with his last motion, the guard grabbed his bleeding throat. Noah eased the body to the ground to avoid a loud thump.

Noah didn't have time for guilt or to watch the blood pool under him. He wiped the blade clean on the guard's pants and holstered it. He turned to unscrew each of the steel drums filled with fuel. When he got to the last one, he heard another shot. Reiter had been seen; he didn't worry about the creature. He knew bullets couldn't kill it. He knew the killing had begun, and Noah had more darkness to bring.

He tipped over the fuel containers just to make sure nothing could be fixed. They spilled gas as he rolled them over the side. They must have fallen far because none made a sound. He turned to the wires that connected the power to the manor. He pulled his knife back out. Noah grabbed the cords where they ran up the wall. They didn't feel powerful, but all the power going to the building and to the lights along the airstrip utilized these cords. Noah knew the Nazi pilots planning to land here who needed these lights were already in the air. They were heading here now from across Germany.

"Fuck you," Noah whispered and pulled his blade through the cords. He got a shock, but he shook it off as total darkness came to the mountain.

# CHAPTER
# THIRTY-THREE

May 1<sup>st</sup> 11:03 PM: Eagle's Nest

KRISTA PUT Alice out of her mind. She closed her eyes and thought about the same things she always did when she was alone. Her nightmares were a horrid combination of Martin's smile when he was a boy, and the list of names of the French she had deported. Von Stülpnagel's signature was on the order, but she was the one who gave him the names. It took her some time to find the right university officials who would hand over the names. The officials that had families at home that they were worried about always talked. She promised their safety in exchange for the names.

She prayed for forgiveness but knew she didn't deserve it. It wasn't until she got the cable telling her about Martin's death that she ever considered the mothers and fathers of the names on that list. *What could she do?* She had joined the party when Hitler sat in jail writing his book.

It wasn't the first time she closed her eyes and held her hands together under her chin and begged God to forgive her.

Then she heard screams around the manor. Screams outside. Shouts and anger. Voices calling for calm. She was afraid to open them, but slowly she raised her eyes and she felt it surprisingly deep and low in her gut. The room was dark, the light had been on, she stood up and flicked the switch up and down. It snapped each time but no light responded. The only light was the small candle she'd lit in the bathroom. She looked under the door and no light came from the hall. She ran to the window and the lights from the airstrip were gone. She saw only darkness outside.

"Damn it," she hated to be right. Something evil was here, it was judgment day... All the bastards who thought they could cleanse Europe. Who were willing to throw Germany into another war, and *they thought it would be different?*

A mist rose up from the darkness below, it seemed to glow as it swirled around just outside her window. Krista couldn't take her eyes off it. She put her hand on the glass, it should've been cold like the mountain air but it radiated heat like an oven coil. The mist swirled until a shape of a person rose from it. The shape was faint like a ghost made of light glowing against the black of night. Time stopped. She thought maybe it was her boy's face. His life flowed into her memory. Krista remembered telling Paul she was pregnant. The first time Martin kicked, waving to his father at his parade, as he sat atop the tank. Martin was raised in the party.

Across the burning hot glass, she saw him, glowing against the darkness. He was shining like a burning wick. Martin, her sweet boy, looked as he did the first time she had dressed him for the Hitler Youth. His hair was perfectly slicked. His hand grazed the glass and then a little tap.

Her view of him blurred slightly as she began to tear up.

"Let me in Mama, it is so cold out here."

She knew it was a trick, she knew it was the devil. She knew the darkness was here to take her to hell. There was no point in running. No point in hiding. It was here to kill her and all the rest. She nodded before she reached up and turned the knob opening the window. The cool air rushed in.

She pushed it open and Martin was gone. A man, tall and thin beyond reason, stood in his place. He looked monstrous, larger than life, he opened his mouth to show her his long fangs. It was the last thing she saw as the creature came inside to consume her.

# CHAPTER
# THIRTY-FOUR

<u>May 1<sup>st</sup> 11:04 PM: Eagle's Nest</u>

ALICE WALKED down the servant stairs and through the kitchen. She didn't want to go outside; it was dangerous, but she knew she had to warn Heinrich. She didn't care what those bastards went through, there was something out there. She froze for a moment and looked at the mess in the kitchen. They were leaving a mess but she knew there was no reason to clean up, it was a stark difference from how organized this kitchen always was.

Machine gun fire. Even in the kitchen, she heard it. Everyone heard that. She stepped out into the stateroom of the manor. The officers were having an animated conversation. They had moved from the bar to the chairs by the fireplace. Eva and the Fuhrer used to sit and listen to the radio there by the fire. When she stepped into the room, Himmler watched her and grew silent. His face was lit by the dying fire. Goring turned from the couch to see her.

"You heard that?" She expected a reaction.

Himmler was impatient. "The men are probably hunting, no one can follow us here."

A single pistol report echoed through the night. Himmler

had intentionally sat in the chair that was the Fuhrer's favorite. He knew exactly where he was sitting.

She raised an eyebrow before she walked to the front door. Her hand hovered by the handle. If there was danger out there, she couldn't go. She wasn't just thinking about herself now.

"Let the soldiers do their job my dear, if we need letters typed, we will be sure to…"

The lights disappeared. She hadn't even noticed the hum of the generator until it was gone. The only light was the orange embers in the fireplace. Schmitt grabbed a piece of wood but they had let the fire go for too long, there was not enough flame to catch on the log. She was right by the windows that went up the length of the door. The power to the lights on the landing strip was gone. Only the burning torches remained.

Alice turned, the best light in the room was the faint moonlight coming in the window. Himmler jumped to his feet. Goring and Schmitt looked as if they had seen ghosts.

"Just an outage," Himmler straightened his uniform. "Schmitt get a soldier down to check the generator."

Schmitt panicked and ran to the door. Alice fell back and hit the wall as she opened the heavy door for him. His boots stomped down the steps and away. She hesitated before looking out into the darkness of the mountain, she was curious but thought better of going out there. Schmitt had disappeared as if the night had swallowed him. She heard him shouting orders. The rest of the officers upstairs in the quarters began to yell for help or answers. The soldiers were shouting orders outside. She couldn't understand them in the panic but she made out certain words. *Bodies, blood everywhere, they've been shot.*

Alice turned back to Himmler. He waved his hand and said something so quiet she didn't hear it. Alice looked at Goring, the drunk had leaked buckets of sweat. Himmler muttered again.

"What?" Alice spoke meekly. He was the new Fuhrer after all.

"Close the damn door!" Himmler yelled and pointed at the door.

Alice slammed it. Himmler pointed desperately at the lock,

Alice turned the deadbolt with a loud snap. The new Fuhrer was so close she could see the sweat on his forehead.

"I thought were safe here my Fuhrer," she whispered.

"I am not afraid!" he shouted, then tried to calm his voice. "The men will take care of it."

They waited by the door. Several minutes passed. The shouting calmed a bit, and their eyes adjusted to the darkness. Alice looked out the window that ran the length of the door frame and focused on the lights from the torches as they were lit one at a time. Watching the airstrip, she hoped to catch a glimpse of Heinrich. She jumped out of her skin when he appeared in the window. Himmler pushed her out of the way and unlocked the door.

Heinrich ignored Himmler and went straight into Alice's arms.

"Report!"

Alice didn't let go. She was so relieved that he was alive.

"Report!" Himmler was angrier this time.

Heinrich pulled from the hug enough to give her a short kiss. He whispered, "just a moment my sweet."

Heinrich turned to Himmler. They had the same first name, but they were so different. Her Heinrich towered over the new Fuhrer. They had worked together, but Himmler was an SS officer and Heinrich was just a sergeant in the German army. Two very different classes.

"We have five dead men, and one missing."

"What?" Alice didn't hide her shock.

Heinrich shook his head. "I think allied commandos but it is impossible to say at this point."

"But the bridge, the mines…It can't be."

Heinrich nodded. "They could've been here waiting, on the mountain."

"Ridiculous."

"How doesn't matter, does it?" Alice spoke softly. Himmler ignored her, he made a fist and appeared to be thinking about what to do.

Alice walked to a cabinet that was deeper in the darkness. She had to feel around but she knew it had candles. She held one up and Heinrich lit it. Himmler now in the glow wiped the sweat off his brow.  Her Heinrich squared his shoulders and looked into her eyes.

"Take the Fuhrer and go to the library, barricade the door, and don't let anyone in unless it is myself or Schmitt."

Goring reached over and grabbed the candle. "I'll take the Fuhrer."

Alice sighed. They were planning to leave her. Her brave Heinrich Hitzinger shook his head. He knew she was acting for their son as much as her.

"Take Alice, she knows this manor better than anyone else here."

She hoped that this was not the last time she would see her Heinrich. She gave him a kiss. Himmler took her candle and walked in the wrong direction.

"Hey, the library is upstairs."

She turned back at the staircase and waited to watch Heinrich step out into the night.

# CHAPTER
# THIRTY-FIVE

THE SCREAMING and yelling by the airstrip had started a few minutes ago and would not stop. The panic when the lights went out was enough to give Mallory a chuckle. The darkness was so complete they saw very little of it. The guards were scared and angry with each other. They watched from a good hiding spot as one of the guards failed to light one of the torches while fumbling a lighter.

Another guard came up behind him. "Dein Hund soll deine Mutter ficken,"

Herzog suppressed a laugh, when the torch was lit the guards ran off. Mallory looked at him. "Did he just say…"

"Your dog fucks your mother, basically."

"What?" Marion looked at them confused.

"They said it not me," Herzog shook his head.

The Germans had no clue what they were dealing with. As the minutes ticked away the officers got quiet inside. The soldiers were scared, they saw the twisted and sucked-dry bodies of two of their friends. They were confused by their friend who went crazy and shot himself and his fellow soldiers.

Reiter wasn't just killing the Nazis; he was driving them mad and making them suffer along the way. This was the reason Field Marshal Brunner had given them for keeping the creature alive.

Every minute or so, Marion would turn over and look at him. War is patience. He had told her that over drinks in France. She was curious and he had hoped she would never find out. They waited for Noah. This was his mission. They had an hour until the planes landed. The Nazis were lighting more torches further away, having to improvise and light the strip.

*That-a-boy,* Mallory thought. Not only had Noah shut it down, the fact that the lights were still off meant he must have made the generator impossible to fix. The next light they would see would be on the eastern horizon. Mallory relaxed until he heard the sound of a woodlark. A common bird song in England. It was a smart warning because when Noah ran up to them, Mallory kept his knife in his holster.

Noah dropped and rolled next to him.

"Well done," Mallory whispered.

"I dumped the fuel."

Marion leaned in. "They have been lighting candles inside, I think Reiter is in."

"What is he waiting for?" Herzog asked.

"He could be working quietly," Noah hoped.

Mallory shook his head. "They lost power to the crank on the pull wire for the landing strip."

Noah sighed. "Just like an aircraft carrier, it is not electric. They will still be able to land."

Mallory nodded, but he didn't like it. He knew they needed to wait it out. He wanted to rush in there but he had a very specific mission that only he and Noah knew about. Hitler had hosted a group of scientists working on super weapons here at the Eagle's Nest. Biological and atomic weapons, he had to find the labs. That had to be his focus.

"We have to talk," Mallory gave him a serious look. "I need to go in there."

"Let the Count do his job," Noah insisted.

"You know what I need to find."

Noah nodded. "I understand but let's hope the Count gets to work."

"Don't worry my friend," Marion didn't sound happy. "He can't control his thirst; those fucking Nazis don't have long now."

# CHAPTER
# THIRTY-SIX

<u>May 1<sup>st</sup> 11:25 PM: Eagle's Nest</u>

ALICE WAS tired of looking at Himmler in the candle glow. Goring had fallen asleep, drooling slightly, and snoring in his chair. They had moved the couch in front of the door. They tipped it at an angle that might stop the door if the intruder didn't put much force into pushing it. Two enlisted soldiers were in the hall guarding the door with machine guns. A tiny bit of orange light was coming from the window where the torches lit the airstrip. She went to the window and watched them for a few minutes. Those tiny flames were so important to save their lives. The soldiers were desperate to keep the flames lit, but the intense high mountain air blew some of them out.

"It is quiet, I told you nothing was out there. They got spooked and shot themselves."

Alice heard Himmler but kept her eyes focused on the flames of the airstrip outside. They heard the footsteps of a child on the ceiling above. Alice's old room was also above the library which meant that Irma and young Josef were just above them. That was a little boy's feet she heard running and playing. Alice remembered the toy Luftwaffe plane he carried. When they heard him run, she imagined that toy plane taking off in his hand. In the silence of the night, they heard the muffled voice of the mother telling her boy to sit still.

Himmler laughed, Alice turned to look at him. *What could possibly be amusing right now?*

He knew what she was wondering. "Sounds like my mother. Heinrich sit down, Heinrich no running in the house. Heinrich…"

"She must've been so proud of you. What you became."

Himmler shook his head. "It doesn't matter."

Alice thought it very much mattered what this man's mother thought of him. Agree with the party or vote for it, it didn't matter. All Germans knew his name now, and they all knew Himmler was a ruthless leader. She wasn't sure what to say to him.

"My Fuhrer," he whispered at first and then raised his voice . "She must've been proud of you, my Fuhrer."

He was serious. She could see in his eyes he very much expected her to say his new title. She never got a chance. There was a scream elsewhere in the building. A man's voice screaming in both terror and pain. It traveled through the walls, and everyone in the manor heard it. Goring even woke up. Another scream, from the other side of the large manor. Alice heard the scurry of the young boy's feet above them.

"The children should be here, my Fuhrer. There are three children at the Nest they should be here in the most secure place."

Himmler was stunned. "There is no threat."

"Then why are we hiding?"

Goring stood up. "Do not speak to the Fuhrer that way."

Alice had heard enough. She couldn't take it anymore; she pushed the couch enough to crack the door. The two soldiers stood in the hall pointing their rifles in the dull light of a single lantern. They couldn't see a thing down the hall.

"One of you men, go find the children and bring them here."

"She doesn't give orders!" Goring yelled from his chair. "Protect the Fuhrer."

Alice grabbed one of the candles and put it on the floor, she squeezed through the door. She reached back to get her light. Once she held up the candle, she saw the fear on the closest soldier's face. The long hall was mostly darkness. She nodded, wanted him to know she understood his fear.

"I am going to get the mothers and the children, don't shoot us by mistake." She pointed to the back staircase. "My name is Alice; I'll tell you I am coming, OK?"

The young man stepped out of her way. Alice walked into the darkness, her candle only lit a small space in front of her. Once in the stairwell, the sounds of panic on the third floor were louder. The voices were in a panic, hard to understand. When she stepped onto the floor a soldier turned and pointed his rifle at her.

"No, no stop I'm German!" She closed her eyes; afraid it was too late.

"Alice!" It was Irma, she was in her doorway. "It is Hitzinger's woman Alice."

The soldier lowered his weapon but he shook like a leaf in a storm. He blocked the open door to Krista's room. He was hard to see in the light from a small lantern now on the floor.

"Krista?"

The soldier blocked the door. She brought the candle closer. He was young, the helmet looked enormous on his head but was strapped tight. Alice had to know what happened to Krista. She pointed with the candle. He patted his chest as if to say *'me first'* and stepped carefully into the room one step ahead of her.

In the orange candle glow, Alice saw something she thought impossible. A puddle of blood, some soaked into the Turkish rug. It wasn't red exactly, crimson liquid mixed with a milk-like bile. At the center of the mess, a human heart soaked in the goo. She knew it was all that remained of Krista.

"Oh my..." the soldier couldn't finish the words. Alice couldn't imagine who would do such a thing, or where Krista's heartless body was now. Then she heard a faint sound.

*Click, click, click...*

It was a familiar sound. She remembered Eva making a joke. *"You see, he has that effect even on puppies."* The Fuhrer used to call Blondie to follow him with that sound.

Alice spun around with the candle, it flickered and the flames almost went out. It suddenly seemed dimmer against the darkness, even in this smaller space. Alice felt it on her skin, like the black parts of night crawled on her. She felt like screaming. She couldn't see where clicking came from.

*Click, click, click...* Again. Closer. *Above?*

"Look up," she told the soldier even when she couldn't. They both silently dared each other over the faint candlelight. She lifted her candle higher and looked up. Impossible. Someone was on the ceiling looking down at them. Before Alice could scream, the figure pounced. Alice dropped the candle in Krista's blood and instantly the light disappeared. The creature from the ceiling landed on the soldier in the fresh darkness. He screamed as Alice ran out of the room.

Now in the light of the hallway lantern, she looked back and saw the creature, it was not a man tearing the helmet off the young soldier like the shell of a peanut. Shock consumed her head to toe, it was something out of myth and the flickering light of the cinema, a creature that lived in the pages of a novel. The monster bit into the soldier's neck just inches away. The dying man screamed but it was too late.

"Alice!" Irma called to her. Alice took a step back and the creature appeared in the door. It looked like a man except for the blood dripping from his chin and lips. He smiled. The teeth were stained red and familiar. The thoughts jumbled together. She had seen the film in Berlin before the war. Bela Lugosi, he was Hungarian but starred in German films. She'd read the novel Dracula soon after on the train back to Berlin after visiting her family in Munich.

Irma grabbed her arm and pulled her backward. Alice looked into the creature's eyes and she felt it reaching out to her mind. It was as if it reached out with hooks and held her in place. She couldn't move but Irma pulled on her. The creature confused her, she only came out of it when she hit the floor of her old room. The pain of landing on her back shook her, but she watched Irma barricade the door with a chair. Josef tried to help her up but the boy was not strong enough.

The door handle rattled, it was just doing it to scare them. It worked. Irma pulled her boy into a hug. Her whole body shook from the terror.

"What the hell the hell was that?"

"Vampire," Alice spoke the words but could hardly believe it.

# CHAPTER
# THIRTY-SEVEN

<u>May 1st 11:30 PM: Eagle's Nest</u>

THE FLICKERING FLAMES of the torches lit the airstrip with a soft orange glow, Heinrich Hitzinger had survived many horrors during the war but this was different. He had to focus on getting them off the mountain. The torches were barely staying lit in the breeze and would likely go out as soon as the planes landed, they would have to light them again each time. Three hundred feet, and they had almost fifty torches to light. They were working as quickly as they could, some of them were just posts with uniform shirts wrapped around them. He had two soldiers working on the generator but the fuel tanks were gone. Even if they could get the hardware fixed, there was no light coming. The only explanation was commandos waiting for them on the mountain. They must've known they were coming and beat them here.

Heinrich Hitzinger taped a flashlight to his M-15 under the barrel. He thought they had enough light on the landing strip, but he was not a pilot. The men were working as fast as they could, they knew this was their only hope of getting out of Germany alive. Survival was all he could think about. Grand words of the new Fatherland rang more hollow with each passing moment.

The manor had finally grown quiet, he should've been focused on the task but he kept looking back. There was a tiny glow from the window of the library. Alice and the new Fuhrer should be safe. Honestly, he never saw a future for him and Alice. He never thought they would escape the bunker. He had been so honored when he was chosen to be in the Fuhrer's detail. He felt relief at the time, which he would never admit to. He thought about his days at the front, Spring in Stalingrad. The fourth wave to enter the city, the nightmares echoed even when he was awake. He was a good warrior, but that came with a price. He knew they couldn't defeat the Russians, and had wanted to die. He'd wanted to die with the Fuhrer.

There were days in the bunker when the bombs kept coming. They all felt desperate, and it started with just holding her hand to comfort her. He held her hand to comfort her, but he felt something too. *They were both going to die, what harm could it cause?* She was beautiful, Hitler probably chose her for that reason as much as her typing. The first time he'd felt guilty, so it was awkward until she unbuttoned his shirt. Her fingers on his skin melted the world away, they were no longer under Berlin. He was only feeling her smooth skin and warmth.

He was supposed to return south to Ingrid and the kids. Maybe they would resettle in the French lands of the greater Reich. It was too painful to think of Russian or American boots stomping on his street in Munich. The Americans would give the Jews Germany to be their eternal Zion just as the Fuhrer had predicted. Ingrid was probably dead, his only surviving child was the one growing in Alice.

It was Himmler who had offered salvation. He needed to be enlisted, an infantryman to pull off his plan. He needed Hitzinger to plan the escape from the bunker. They couldn't tell the Fuhrer because he would never leave German soil again. They would re-settle in the new Fatherland. He would go with Alice. He loved her too, but it was different. She insisted their child was a boy, and he agreed. He had a feeling about their son. He would be a leader.

He had fifteen men on the strip, the torches were creating

warmth, and he even felt a little sweat forming under his collar. Their orders were to protect the tripwire at all costs. If the trip-wire didn't catch the plane and slow it down there would be no landing. Heinrich looked up towards the moon and the stars and wished he could will time to move faster. He had to believe the planes had not been shot out of the air. That they were on their way. That they were out there in the night.

*What if the planes never come?*

He didn't have time to ponder it. Screams came from the manor. All the soldiers turned. In the moonlight, the manor looked lifeless, but the sound of chaos leaked into the night again. He waved at four soldiers to follow him. The rest wanted to run toward the screams. He understood.

"Stay here, protect the trip wire!"

He ran toward the building and it was hard to locate the screams. The shouts came from around the building. "Second floor, protect the library!" he didn't want to shout too loud and warn whoever was in there, or to give away his selfish reasons. He had no choice. They stepped inside and lifted their rifles. No one was in the living room, the fireplace had gone out. Only the faint moonlight from the windows cut the darkness.

"Stay behind me," he called out as he turned the flashlight on. He had fought on both the Eastern and Western fronts. He had earned an Iron Cross at Stalingrad. Boorman and Himmler chose him personally to protect the Fuhrer, the honor of his life. He survived under Berlin being hammered by Russian bombs and it was the worst dread he'd ever felt. Something hit him as he walked into the Nest. It was like an icy hand had grabbed his heart. He hesitated at the bottom of the grand staircase that went to the second floor.

"Sir?" One of the men tried to get his attention. He must not feel it, Heinrich told himself.

Heinrich didn't answer. He lifted his rifle and pointed his light up the staircase to the stained glass with the eagle's crest. Ingrid. His wife stood there in the dress she wore on their wedding day. Her long blonde hair danced at her shoulders. She smiled softly, unaffected by the bright spotlight.

"No!" Heinrich stepped back, the spotlight bounced around and when he pointed it again, she was gone. "No, No!"

"Sir?" The soldier was confused. There were screams coming from upstairs, Heinrich barely heard them.

"Did you see her?" he begged.

The junior infantry officer looked confused. "See who?"

"No, no, I saw her." Heinrich seemed to ignore the screams coming from the third floor. The terror-stricken soldiers stood below him in confusion.

"Sir, the screams," a third soldier insisted.

Heinrich nodded and ran up the stairs, when he shined his light toward the library, he saw the two frightened guards. "It's upstairs!"

"It?" One of the soldiers behind him spoke.

Heinrich waved them to the stairwell, the screams of terror were coming from above and below. All four of them looked down and back up. Heinrich thought it was a trick. His heart almost pounded out of his chest; he wasn't sure which way to go. A wind blew through the stairwell and knocked him back like a tornado. He thought he smelled Stalingrad, the air over that city had felt solid, a thick misery that you could pull into your lungs and choke on.

It stopped him, the feeling of his darkest moments. He had to get past it, and push through the stairwell door like a drowning man coming to the surface. Lit only from the end of his barrel, the hallway was littered with bodies, but he focused on the movement. A man aggressively shook the door handle to one of the rooms. He was not in uniform, Heinrich pointed his rifle and the light seemed to shock him.

"Stop! Hands up or I'll..."

The man turned and hissed at the light like a cornered fox. Heinrich wanted to run but couldn't. He showed blood-stained fangs before he launched into the air and out of the light. Heinrich lifted the rifle to shoot at the ceiling when he heard a whisper, it tickled like it was inside his ear.

"Henri."

Heinrich jumped around to the sound of his wife Ingrid. The creature, he doubted now that it was a man, pounced on his soldier behind him. A soldier whose name he had not bothered to learn. Machine guns fired behind him but Heinrich was too shocked, so he crawled back across the hardwood floor away from the violence. If he were to aim, he'd have to see it and he was too scared. He had to look away. The creature took down one of his men as a lion would a Zebra.

"Who is she, Henri?" Ingrid's voice rattled in his brain.

Heinrich dragged his rifle across the floor, hearing her voice again. He had to look. *How could she be here? What kind of trickery was this?* He looked up and saw that it was not Ingrid. The soldier boy drained of life hit the floor in front of him, the creature stood over the body, impossibly large. It appeared as a man, but it was not. Heinrich closed his eyes and accepted his death. He felt arms under him, someone pulled him backwards across the floor. He desperately fought, thinking the arms would tear him apart.

"Stand up!" He heard Alice's voice but he wasn't sure it was her, another trick?

She pulled with a strength he didn't know she had. He pushed with his feet and they fell back together through a cracked door. Heinrich knew Alice was supposed to be in the library downstairs. *It had to be a trick!* He struggled against her grip. The door shut and he was trapped. He reached for the door.

"No!"

"Heinrich no! Please."

Heinrich scrambled to the door, desperate to get out. As soon as his hand touched the handle, he heard the creature on the other side roar. The wood frame of the door rattled as if the earth had quaked. He closed his eyes, there was nowhere to go. Burning fear traveled the length of his body. He closed his eyes and waited for the end to take him.

Hands pulled him back and when he finally opened his eyes, Alice and Irma had blockaded the door with a couch. The door buckled as something beat on it.

*Henri. Open the door, Henri. I love you.*

In the chaos, the voice was soft, sweet, and comforting.

"Ingrid," Heinrich whispered. He cried into his fist as the creature stopped pounding on the door.

*Open the door, Henri.* The voice was not even a whisper, it was a feeling that crawled in his mind and squeezed his heart.

"What the fuck did he say?" Alice asked.

Irma was standing over the man who was trying to compose himself. "He said, Ingrid."

Through tear-soaked eyes, he saw Alice's disappointment. She knew his wife's name although they never spoke of it. Their accounts of their lives before the bunker were always minus any details of previous marriages or lovers.

"Who is Ingrid?" Irma asked. No one answered her.

"Are you real Alice? Why are you not with the Fuhrer in the library?"

Alice leaned down and kissed him. "I'm real."

Heinrich turned again to see the scared face of 6-year-old Josef whom he remembered from the truck. He suddenly felt watched, embarrassed. He wanted to be strong for the boy, for Alice but he had no strength to call on. The voice of his wife still echoed in his ear.

*Who is she?*

"It plays with your mind," Irma the young mother whispered not wanting her son to hear her.

Heinrich tried to catch his breath. "The Allies have a new weapon."

Alice nodded. "Yes, they have a vampire."

# CHAPTER
# THIRTY-EIGHT

THE SOLDIER'S MIND CRUMBLED. Reiter wormed inside and projected Hitzinger's wife. He whispered in her voice. He urged the soldier to open the door. Hitzinger loved his wife and Reiter could feel the man's desire to run to the voice. Even though he knew it was a trick, he wanted desperately to believe. His mind was a more complicated map of misery than many of the officers. He had survived battles and been in bunkers with their glorious leader. The woman with a child didn't have guilt close to the surface like most of the Nazis. The mother was less complicated. She loved her boy, but she had done terrible things, and he could see it all. The memories were close to the surface like a book left open for him to read tales of her guilt and transgressions.

He put his hands on the doors and reached into their minds at the same time. They were too afraid to open the door. That was good, as the reinforcements were coming. Reiter sensed them coming on two fronts. The officers scattered around the building had decided to fight. Doors were opening and despite the darkness, they were coming for him. A few were still hiding. The soldiers guarding the strip had their rifles ready and were advancing on the manor as if they were facing an army.

*Too bad for them they were not.*

A door opened behind him and Reiter rose quickly to the ceiling. An SS officer stepped into the hall with his pistol. His fear flared when he saw the dead soldiers scattered on the floor. Reiter dropped onto him and stuck his claws into his throat. The officer gagged and struggled as more Nazis came out of the stairwell. Reiter used the officer in his grip as a shield and the body absorbed several bullets as he approached the new attackers. They came through the door and Reiter confronted them.

He reached in and cracked open his chest plate, the Nazi screamed as Reiter reached in and pulled. With his last breath the soldier saw his own heart beat for the final time. The soldier collapsed and Reiter held the organ for the other Nazis to see. One of them stepped backwards as Reiter squeezed the heart, the blood draining down his arm. For a moment they were frozen in fear.

Reiter focused on the officer, shaking in his polished boots and neatly pressed SS uniform. Any commander's bluster the man might have had drained out of him before he turned back to run toward the stairwell. Four soldiers blocked his escape. Reiter grabbed the officer and pushed him toward the stairwell, the Nazis fell back and Reiter rode on his back down the steps like a sled down a snowcapped hill, breaking his face against each one of the steps. The soldiers toppled like dominoes, and the last one hit his head on the second-floor landing.

Reiter spun as fast as he could. It was a blur, some attacked, others ran. His body urged him to consume their blood, the hunger burned inside him. He resisted it; he was leaving these Nazis dead on this mountain. He would not turn a single one of them. Those he consumed he must take the time to destroy.

He stepped out onto the landing in front of the garish eagle crest stained glass window and stood in the faint moonlight that shined through. Behind a shining flashlight, an entire squad of Nazi soldiers poured in the front door. They stopped and looked up at him, more than a dozen bullets were shifted into the firing chambers, the barrels pointed at his shape. They couldn't see him fully. He reached out to their minds; fear was the open door, and he came through. They all had mothers so he reached in and appeared as such.

"My boy..." he spoke in more than a dozen voices.

They all heard it. It only bought him a few seconds. Some of them hated their mothers. The rifles were raised and the shots rang out. Reiter rose through the air and spun. He felt a few of the bullets travel through him. To him they were like bee stings. He landed in the middle of the squad. Just as the man he held fired, he spun him around. The bullets tore through the soldiers. Blood splashed on Reiter, he licked it off his lips and felt the wounds on his body healing. He knocked the rifle out of the arms of the man he used to fire. He bit into him and the soldier's memories rushed over him like a wave.

His name was Wilhelm, he rode into Stalingrad on the eastern front with the 4th Panzer division. Throughout most of 1942, he fought to claim the city alongside a squad with more Italians and Spaniards than Germans. They were confident they could turn the tide of the battle. When 1943 arrived, they were out of ammunition and went days without eating. When the deal was made to end the battle, they were allowed to retreat. Wilhelm was a sergeant and given command of the 7th Panzer Tank division, with orders only to return to Germany.

Late into the spring, they traveled back home. They were filled with pent-up rage and punished any Russians they could find along the way. Tearing apart small villages became a sport. The smaller ones had no way to report them, and the Soviets had larger issues of concern. Wilhelm himself suggested they burned the fields as they retreated. They left starvation in their wake.

Reiter looked into the eyes of the man guilty of this crime as life left his body. He didn't see much in the way of humanity, only fear of dying.

"Bastard," Reiter whispered and broke his neck. The front door to the manor opened again slowly. Just outside, two squads were gathered. He waved them closer.

# CHAPTER
# THIRTY-NINE

<u>May 1<sup>st</sup> 11:45 PM: Eagle's Nest</u>

THE GUNFIRE and screams continued beyond their barricaded door. Irma held Josef close to her, she covered his exposed ear. Still, the boy cried. Alice couldn't blame him. The battle had raged for ten minutes. They had one candle flickering almost to nothingness, just a wick floating in melted wax. It seemed unnaturally fast, but the world ceased to make sense. They would only have moonlight from the window soon enough. Alice was silent through the whole thing; she shook against Heinrich and he hugged her. They listened to the battle trying to make sense of what they could only hear.

The gunfire stopped. After a few moments of silence, she looked at Heinrich. The confident veteran of the front lines was reduced to a shell of himself. He was afraid to get up. Alice turned and looked at him. She had never seen him this way, even after months of bombings, living in the bunker with the Russians coming.

"We need to make a plan."

Heinrich looked away, pained to admit what he was thinking. "A vampire."

Irma held her son a little tighter as she spoke. "Impossible."

"You saw what it did." Alice looked up at the ceiling looking for strength. "We know it is not natural, we know it is a monster."

"Fairy tales," Irma was rattled just as they were. "Just things of books and the picture houses, Count Dracula is not real."

"I read it in school," Alice took a deep breath. "It has been a while but it makes sense. It drinks blood and has fangs. It controls minds like Dracula did Renfield."

"Renfield?" Heinrich was confused.

"It doesn't matter," Alice pulled away from Heinrich. "It is a vampire and we know a few things about him. We have to fight it."

"Have you not heard what was going on down there? What chance do we have?" Irma didn't mask her fear. Alice understood that she had shown strength for her boy. Irma had gone from disbelief to fear, slowly accepting the truth.

Alice reached into her shirt and pulled out her necklace. She had two pieces hanging from it, one was an eagle pendant given to her on her birthday from Eva and the Fuhrer. The other was a cross her mother gave her on her 16th birthday.

"It is blessed, we hold it against him," Alice held up the cross in the candlelight. "We ask God to spare us."

Irma and Heinrich shared a look, in a less tense moment they might have laughed at her.

"Working for the Fuhrer, I am glad you were spared much of the horror of this war," Irma smirked. "I am not sure God wants to hear from us."

Alice understood, they thought her position with the Fuhrer had shielded her from the reality of the war, she expected Heinrich to defend her but he didn't. She had typed Hitler's letters and speeches, she knew more details of the war than a secretary should. Heinrich looked away; he had been calling out to the woman he claimed was dead. Alice snapped her fingers to get his attention.

"Do we have a reason to survive?" Alice asked him. He looked back at her confused. "Your son and I? Do we have a reason to get to that airstrip?"

Heinrich nodded and slung his machine gun over his shoulder. He was trying to summon strength. "For the new Fatherland."

Footsteps. Loud, intentionally booming steps coming up from the nearby stairwell. The monster wanted them to know he had returned. Alice turned to see Josef sitting near the candle as if the light was a bubble that could protect him. Alice turned and it was too late...

# CHAPTER
# FORTY

May 1<sup>st</sup> 11:48 PM: Eagle's Nest

HE REACHED out to Irma's mind as he rose over the stairwell. The Nazis littered the floor. There was one Nazi he couldn't let go. He stopped at the door. He smelled the blood of four scared humans, but the one he wanted was holding her child tight to her body.

"Judgment day Irma," Reiter whispered as he touched the door with the palm of his hand. His mind traveled through the thin piece of wood. He crawled across the memories, as real as the day she lived them. Young and a mother, widowed by the war, she took the job because her son needed her to. It was easy, now that the Allies were taking back Europe, to tell herself she was different, but Irma supported the Reich to her core. She hated Jews, Communists, and anyone else who she thought drained the system.

After she lost her husband, it was easy to let the anger drive her. Her parents suffered because the Jews ruined Germany, her father went to jail with Hitler. Fraud elections, the government tried to cheat the Fuhrer of his rights. He had to take Germany back. If they didn't kill the Jews, Communists, or traitors then they would be crushed even further than they were after the Great War.

She believed in her mission. The filth would go into those chambers or it would be Germany and the entire civilized world that would die instead. If they wouldn't go into the chambers, she had a stick she hit their knees with. She carried the stick everywhere. When the Field Marshal promoted her to SS, they gave her a cane with a silver skull on it. Himmler himself called her the Cold Stone and said he wished every camp had one of her.

She was surprised by their faith in her, and the promotion. The truth was, she was happy to do the jobs no one else wanted to do. Each time she shut the door of the chamber at Auschwitz she felt relief. It was hard work, and the smell was terrible, but she believed it was the best thing for Josef and his generation. She wanted his children to never know a mixed and dirty Europe.

She looked into the faces of thousands of men, women, and children before ending their lives. She only felt guilty because the war was ending and she couldn't continue. She had turned her own pain and anger into mass cruelty. Reiter felt her confusion but he had none.

*Open the door, Irma. Open the door.*

# CHAPTER
# FORTY-ONE

May 1st 11:50 PM: Eagle's Nest

ALICE CLOSED her eyes for just a moment. She held Heinrich's hand, and tried to stay quiet. She worried the vampire could hear her heart beating. She opened her eyes and fought back a scream. Irma walked slowly toward the door, her hand outstretched toward the handle.

"Irma sit down!" Alice whispered, on the verge of a desperate scream. "Irma, please."

Henrich jumped up and shook her, the woman stopped but looked past him.

"You won't feel a thing," she droned.

"He is in her mind, it's too late," Alice knew, being quiet or hiding couldn't save them. She walked to the wooden chair at the desk, she lifted it in the air smashed it on the floor. She picked up two wooded chair legs and offered Heinrich one. He was shocked. She pointed at her own heart, then at the knife he carried on his waist. He pulled out his blade and started to scrape it into a sharp point.

Alice turned to see Irma pushing the couch.

"No! Irma!" Alice ran to tackle her but Irma pushed her away easily. Alice rolled on the floor "Take Josef!"

Alice heard the couch scrape across the floor, and the door open. He was here.

Alice reached up and pulled at Irma's ankle. She was entranced and heard nothing but the call to open the door. Heinrich wasn't even close to finishing his stake. Alice watched the door open in terror. The world slowed in that moment as the vampire appeared. Yellow inhuman eyes locked with hers. Irma tipped her head, presenting her neck to him.

"No! Mommy!" Her boy pleaded behind Alice.

She couldn't watch, her eyes closed as the vampire bit into Irma instantly, she screamed in pain, the spell broken. His teeth clenched deeply into her skin. Irma was caught in the bite like a gazelle in the grip of a lion. Alice only had seconds to act, she grabbed Irma's shoulders and threw her to the ground. The creature was attached to her neck and fell with her to the ground. They had to move.

Alice ran through the door. Heinrich pulled Josef with him. Alice was the first to scream at the sight of the carnage left in the hall. Alice scooped up the boy even as he cried for his mother. She hugged him tight against her body and ran for the stairs dodging the human debris. The building was as dark as could be, her feet kept hitting bodies that she couldn't see, and she had no choice but to step on them.

Heinrich turned and unloaded his machine gun into the room. The vampire wailed—it was not pain but a war cry. When she got to the landing under the stained-glass Eagle's crest, it was smashed and broken in pieces, the mountain air blew her hair. Josef hugged her tight and wept.

"It's OK, It's OK," she lied to the boy. *What choice did she have?*

The moon shined through the broken glass and more bodies filled the space, an SS officer lay at her feet coughing and hacking blood. The dying man reached for her and she felt his fingernail on her ankle.

"Run!" The dying man tried to say as he choked on blood.

"Where are the other two children?"

The dying officer pointed to the kitchen. Alice ran into the room and whispered. "Children?"

A cabinet slid open and a little boy, maybe five years old,

crawled out holding the hand of his sister who looked a year younger. Alice let Josef down, she leaned down to pull them into a hug. She wished that she could save them, she prayed that she could. They pleaded for their parents.

"Shush, we need to go, we're in danger, you need to be quiet and follow me."

"Miss Alice will protect us," Josef told them.

She held his hand in her left, and she fit the other children's hands in her right. It was awkward but they stepped out to look for Heinrich. He came down and looked at her with wide eyes. "The plane will be here in forty minutes, take the children, and wait at the airstrip."

"Where are you going?"

"To save the Fuhrer!"

# CHAPTER
# FORTY-TWO

MALLORY LEANED up against a tree and was transfixed, watching the show. He wasn't a fan of the Germans from the last war, but surviving the blitz had intensified his hatred. He watched them running in panic and listened to them scream. He would never deny enjoying it. The Count cut them down quickly, as soon as one scream ended, another echoed in the mountain air. Each wave of soldiers that went into the building set off more screams. He almost laughed at the last group; Reiter didn't even play with them. The screams of pain started almost instantly.

Marion lay in the grass nearby and was not as amused. The ground was cold and hard. Herzog and Noah both kept low, they were also enjoying the show. Noah appeared focused and stoic, although he had a slight smirk. Mallory turned to watch the airstrip. The soldiers near the strip were down to a dozen men, and they were hearing all of it. It had taken so many of their soldiers to light the torches and now most of them had gone into the building to try to fend off the assault. Who knew how many were dead, how many were still hiding?

"Less than an hour till the planes start landing," Noah whispered. It was becoming unlikely that the planes would be able to land. In a panic, the Nazis might try to escape back down the mountain. Mallory couldn't let any sensitive materials or secret weapons plans make it off this mountain. Only He and Noah knew about this part of the mission, and the responsibility was all his.

"Landing those planes will be a tough order, we need to make sure the Count doesn't miss anyone."

"He's doing his job, you ready to do yours?"

Mallory didn't have time to respond. A window smashed on the side of the building, Mallory rolled over. Staying low, he moved in to get a view. He watched someone jump out of a first-floor window and land with a harsh thud. Noah followed Mallory and they shared a look.

"Oh no you don't," Mallory smiled at Noah and unhooked the holster holding his pistol. The two men moved through the trees toward the escaping man. Mallory inched closer, he was almost in reach as the Nazi tried to get up. He was injured, his foot twisted unnaturally from his ankle, he bit down on his sleeve to keep from screaming. Mallory could now see even in the darkness that the Nazi was an SS officer.

He fell back and grabbed at his ankle as if he could make the pain disappear. He looked up into the trees and prayed to whatever Nazis believed in. When the SS officer opened his eyes, he stared into the barrel of Mallory's Colt 1911. Mallory pulled the hammer back with his thumb.

"I don't have to tell a smart officer like you to shut your trap, do I?"

The sweat-soaked officer may have been a stud when the party formed fifteen years ago, he had power but he had never faced a gun like this in the entirety of the war. Now he was a slightly thick, balding man middle-aged man. Mallory knew their ranks, the symbol of the three-pointed leaf. Reichsführer, a national leader, he guessed he was in the Fuhrer or Himmler's orbit.

"You can talk, just no screaming," Noah said from the darkness out of the Nazi's sight. He only stared up at Mallory and the barrel of his pistol.

"What hell did you unleash on us?" The officer spoke in heavily accented English.

Mallory chuckled. "That is rich coming from your kind."

"There are children in there, three children, they don't deserve whatever is happening."

"We can't stop the wrath of God," Noah leaned closer. The Nazi clearly saw his Jewish features. Mallory saw the reaction "You brought them to this mountain."

"I am just a secretary," the Reichsfuhrer lied. His English was better than his lies.

"You're lying, my Jewish friend here is going to tell me your name."

Noah leaned closer to his face and shuffled a deck of cards. On one side they had standard poker symbols, and on the other, black and white photos of SS officers. He shuffled through three cards. He drew the third and he held it right by the Nazi's face.

"Do we have a match?"

"Indeed, not a secretary," Noah stood back up and showed Mallory the card. "Franz Deluge."

"Ohhh," Mallory grinned. "I know you, Franz, by reputation only of course."

"There is a mistake my name is…"

"Franz, we know you." Mallory crouched down closer. "Head of the national police, you enforced loyalty so don't grovel on the last night of your Reich."

A realization came over Franz. He was about to die, begging or lying wouldn't change anything. Mallory didn't know the details as well as Noah, but Franz was behind an early purge of Communists and Jews that were in the old government. This was a big fish they found struggling on their hook. The only hope for this piece of shit was making a deal. He probably knew that was not going to work either.

"Jew rat. Limey bastard, get it over with."

"Well," Mallory nodded. "Franz my boy we can make this quick as it needs to be or…"

Franz turned back to the manor at the sound of screams.

"Talk to us about the location of the science labs in the manor or we will throw you back to our friend inside."

Franz grit his teeth. The thought of it was far worse than

dying quickly by a bullet. He was in pain and wanted the escape desperately.

"He is actually thinking about it?" Noah joked.

"Alright Franz, on your feet soldier, you're going back..." Mallory pointed at the manor.

"Wait, wait." Franz looked back at the manor and a fresh wave of screams escaped the building. "You'll kill me right here. You promise?"

"Where are the labs?" Mallory wasn't debating.

"Behind the library, there is a copy of Alice in Wonderland. German translation. Pull from the shelf, it will open."

Mallory looked up at Noah. "A hidden lab, cute"

"I can be very useful to the Allies," Franz begged.

"You know Franz," Mallory smiled. "Yesterday that might have meant something, but tonight."

Mallory snapped his fingers. Noah put a gag in his mouth. Franz tried to scream as it got knotted behind his head. It was impossible for the irony of this moment to escape them. In his role as Reichfuhrer of the national police, how many people were marched to their death based on his orders? Under the gag, he tried to beg.

"We can't hear you, Franz, begging time is over." Noah walked him to the cliff edge. Each step brought agonizing pain to the man's broken ankle. Mallory followed behind and heard footsteps behind him. Marion and Herzog trailed them.

"What is he doing?" Marion stopped short of Mallory who blocked her path. "There is no reason to play games with him, why torture the guy?"

"No reason? Are you serious?" Herzog shook his head.

"That man delighted in causing pain, don't feel sorry for him," Noah said just before he pushed Franz off the cliff. There were a few beats of silence and then they faintly heard his body bounce off the rock face twice.

"He said there were children," Marion looked at Noah as he returned. "That is where I draw the line."

Noah didn't seem happy about this. He took a deep breath. "I didn't expect them to bring families."

"But they did, and those kids are not guilty."

Noah looked around at all the eyes staring at him. Mallory

knew Marion was right and hoped that Noah's heart had not gotten so hard that they wouldn't have a debate on the issue. They both knew this would cause both of them serious headaches. *Where would the children go?* They would solve it, Mallory was sure of it.

"Fair enough, but only children return with us."

# CHAPTER
# FORTY-THREE

May 1<sup>st</sup> 11:55 PM: Eagle's Nest

JOSEF GRIPPED ALICE'S hand as tightly as the young boy could. Alice leaned down to look the other boy in the eye. Both the new children were blonde-haired and blue-eyed and she suspected they looked like copies of one of their parents. They were so scared that they shook. Alice smiled at them, trying despite the carnage around them to calm them down.

"I'm Alice, what are your names?"

"Robert," the boy said.

"Thea," the young girl whispered.

Alice almost asked her to repeat herself because she barely heard her. "I'm sorry we don't have time to find your parents."

Robert said something but Alice couldn't hear him over the roar of the vampire and the sound of a machine gun. Alice prayed that it wasn't Heinrich.

She pulled the children forward into an awkward run. "Hold your sister's hand tight Robert, no matter what you see or hear don't let go."

The boy nodded. There was a series of screams that came from upstairs. Alice pulled them toward the open front door. The soldiers had left it ajar. The kids screamed as they ran down the front steps of the manor. It was Josef who shushed them. Alice kept her eyes on the burning torches of the airstrip.

When they hit the gravel of the drive, Alice picked up her pace and dragged the kids. Her heart beat out of her chest. *She had lived through the invasion and now this?* There was a whistling sound behind her, approaching from above. She knew that sound, British thunderbolt planes. That whining whistle tore through the sky just before the bombs hit.

Alice pulled the kids to the ground and covered their heads. The whistling faded. Alice opened her eyes and a boot was inches from her face. It wasn't a German boot. She didn't know whose it was. She closed her eyes. She wished she could save the children, give birth and hold her boy. This seemed to be the end. She felt the tears building up. She ground her teeth for the last moment.

"Do it, quickly." She didn't mean to speak. She pulled the children into a hug.

*Would it hurt she wondered?* She heard the screams, so she steeled herself for pain. What more could the Allies take from her at this point? She laid her face across the gravel and accepted it. She prayed.

*Please God make it quick.*

"We are not savages, open your eyes." The German was rough but passable, but it was that awkward way Brits spoke the language.

The tip of the combat boot tapped her forehead.

"Open up," That was English. An American accent this time.

Alice listened and gasped, the children were still crying. She had to be strong for them, even though she wanted to keep her face in the gravel. The children grabbed her hands again. Alice let go long enough to roll on her back and look up. She only saw the Jewish face for a moment before the American pistol took up her vision.

"Let go and we'll take the children." The Jew spoke better German than the Brit. Alice looked around the Brit, a woman who was dressed for battle and another man who looked German. The children gripped her hand tighter.

"It is OK we are not going to hurt you," The woman who was dressed like a commando spoke softly to reassure the children. They didn't understand English. Josef buried his head into Alice's shoulder. The traitor translated. His accent was Low German, he was from the north.

"Please, I need to protect the children. I'm not an officer. I am just this boy's mother."

Alice prayed that Josef followed her lie. She was just a secretary, but she had a feeling that didn't matter to them. She could see their faces judging her as if she had started the war. The light from the airstrip was the brightest she had seen it since the attack began. She saw their faces clearly. The Jew leaned closer, just over her. She felt his beady eyes looking over her.

He pulled out a deck of playing cards. He seemed to shuffle them. She watched, wondering what the hell he was doing. He pulled a card.

"Ahhh there we go. Two of diamonds."

She saw the two of diamonds get closer as the Jew held the card beside her face.

"Nice to meet you, Alice Von Vogt."

Hearing her name was a punch in the gut, tears formed. She was desperate. She felt like a rope was slipping from her hands. *Say anything!*

"I'm just a mother, please don't hurt my children."

"No one is hurting kids," said the Brit.

"Alice," the Jew smiled. The bastard smiled at her misery. "You worked for the Fuhrer, didn't you?"

"I'm just a mother, please listen I…"

The Jew turned the card around slowly and there she was—the portrait that the Fuhrer had commissioned for all his staff. Taken in Berlin by the official Reich photographer. She had her hair done by Eva's personal hairdresser and wore the same suit and shirt the Fuhrer picked for them to wear at rallies. Tears leaked down her face. She had been so proud that day. Eva gave prints to all the staff, she sent one home and it was probably still framed on the mantle back home in Munich.

*She had no idea that picture would get her killed.*

"I'm just a typist, I swear."

"Sure thing lass," the Brit said.

"Important enough to travel with the Fuhrer," the Jew raised an eyebrow. "And tell me, why is a typist here?"

"She is pregnant." The voice echoed strangely in the air. They turned to see it. Wearing a Nazi trench coat as a cape and looking as if Bela Lugosi had stepped off the screen, the vampire was there. Alice thought for a moment she saw someone different, it was only a flash: her father, and then the Fuhrer himself. Then the caped vampire was back.

"I don't care." The Jew dismissed him. Of course, the thoughtless rat didn't care about her. If she could rip out his heart she would.

"Take her with the children, it is not her child's fault." The vampire spoke before fading into the darkness. When it was gone the air felt lighter.

"Plenty of time, for justice my friend," said the Brit.

The Jew never took his eyes off her even when speaking to his team. "Mallory you, have a mission. Herzog, they are your prisoners."

She couldn't feel safe, not yet. "What have you unleashed on us?"

"I'm glad you asked Alice," the Jew grinned. "Not enough, what we unleashed is not enough but I prayed for wrath, it was the best we were given."

# CHAPTER
# FORTY-FOUR

THE ONLY SOUND Heinrich heard as he walked down the long dark hall was blood dripping. It was a sound no one should recognize, and before his years in the war, he never would have His boots stuck to the floor as he stepped through pools of blood.

There was also the slight rattle of the M-15. It wasn't his, he'd grabbed it off a dead soldier. It wasn't well maintained, with signs of rust and a long history of deployment. Still, this weapon probably killed plenty of Allies and had more work to do. He couldn't see anything; it was slow-moving, and his boots ran into bodies every few feet. The darkness was so complete he wasn't even sure he was going in the right direction.

A bell chimed. The library clock struck midnight, he'd heard it marking seven o'clock earlier. He followed the deep tones of the clock. It was loud enough that on quiet nights he was sure it was heard throughout the manor. Heinrich got to the end of the hall and ran into the door as the last chime echoed.

He tested the handle, it was locked. Feet shuffled on the other side. A faint candle glow leaked from under the door. He wanted to call out to the Fuhrer, but what if it was behind him.

He looked over his shoulder into the darkness, he didn't see anyone, but the vampire could be hiding. It could be waiting for him to open the door. He tapped lightly; he summoned all the strength he had just to whisper.

"Reichfuhrer?" There was no answer. He had to speak a little louder. "It is Sergeant Hitzinger, I am here to protect you."

He heard feet shuffling again on the other side. He didn't want to show them how afraid he was. He needed to show the new Fuhrer his strength.

"Please open the door my Fuhrer."

"How do I know it is you?" It was Himmler.

Heinrich leaned his head against the door. He couldn't die here begging for Himmler to open the door. He had to admit the truth. It could be a trick, the creature used voices inside your mind. How else could he have seen Ingrid? The vampire would never admit to his tricks.

"You don't, nothing in your mind is safe you understand?"

There was silence for a moment. Then another voice. Goring. "You can't open it."

Heinrich hit the door. "Damn it, Goring. Shut your mouth, you drunk bastard."

The door opened and Himmler reached out to pull him in. Heinrich turned around and pointed his rifle at the darkness. The faint glow of the candle lighting the library finally lit the hall, he expected to see the vampire there pouncing, but the level of devastation, and the number of dead in the hall was shocking.

Goring cursed, Himmler pulled him inside, and Heinrich shut the door and turned the deadbolt. He immediately positioned a chair under the handle.

Heinrich turned and looked around the room. He felt relieved to have even faint light as well as an urge to salute the grandfather clock by the bookshelf that led him here. Heinrich took a look at the two officers and they looked sweaty but untouched. He saw the glow in the window coming from the airstrip torches and felt a wave of relief.

"What the hell happened out there?"

Heinrich stood on an edge here. He knew what he saw, but they didn't see it. *Would they believe him or dismiss him as crazy?*

*He had to believe that they heard it all happening outside their door, how could they think something natural was happening?*

"I know how it sounds, but…"

"A vampire," Himmler looked away out the window. "Romanian, his name is Count Reiter."

Goring and Heinrich looked at him stunned.

"The truth." Himmler paced, clearly thinking about what to say. "It has been some time since the war has been going well. We have been desperate for any advantage. We explored many myths and legends looking for advantages."

"What advantages?"

"Sergeant Hitzinger, we are fighting for the soul of the Reich. You see what Jews have done to Europe. This war is ultimately their fault."

Heinrich didn't want to debate. "What advantages?"

Himmler looked at the flame as he spoke. "The Reiter castle is on the highest peak in Romania, it has sat above the most strategic passes in the country, key to protecting or taking one of the most valuable regions of Europe. The Turks tried for centuries to take the castle and they never could. They sent great warriors and even armies, the Reiter castle never fell in hundreds of years of sieges."

"Reiter is not human." Heinrich nodded.

"We thought it was a fairy tale," Himmler grinned. "Meant to scare off the children, but there are no children at the top of a peak like that. It was meant to scare off armies."

"It didn't work, did it?"

Himmler sighed. "It had slept for centuries. A vampire was a tempting weapon."

Heinrich shook his head. "You pissed it off."

Tapping, just a finger nail lightly on the outside of the door. The three turned toward the library door. Hitzinger put his finger up to silence them. *Was it in their mind? No one moved.*

Himmler swallowed and pointed out the window. "Forty-five minutes, the first plane will land."

"We are not going to need more than that first plane."

Goring closed his eyes tightly in frustration. "We will get on that plane Sergeant; we believe in you."

# CHAPTER
# FORTY-FIVE

May 2nd 12:20 AM Eagle's Nest

REITER HAD his hand on the door and listened to the Nazi bastard tell his story. The amount of fear they were feeling helped pump their blood quickly around their body. The minutes were getting shorter towards the time when the plane was meant to land. They were nervously watching the clock tick away closer to the time when they had to open the door. Reiter understood this was the most important of the Nazis still alive.

He had killed more than a hundred of them but who was counting. Noah would make sure that the Nazis never left this mountain. Once the last remaining Nazis were dead, he would have to deal with Marion Riverwood. She was the most determined to kill him. She and Noah both carried wooden stakes, from trees fallen on his mountain in Romania.

The only human part of him that remained was the heart. The curse could only be broken when the stake pierced his heart. He didn't make the rules or understand why. The theory was that the wood from his own land was needed to complete his death. That it was the mountain that ultimately killed him.

A part of him wanted that to happen, but the allure of the

dream, and the stolen memories. He could live forever in those realities and never grow tired. He just had to finish this mission and go home.

Reiter tapped on the door lightly with his fingernail. "Come on Reichfuhrer," he whispered in German. "Open the door."

# CHAPTER
# FORTY-SIX

<u>May 2nd 12:25 AM: outside of the Eagle's Nest</u>

MARION KEPT her Ruby pistol in her hand and her eyes on Alice the entire time. The Nazi woman was content to sit with the children crowding her lap. They sat leaned up against a tree. Away from the manor and a little distance from the airstrip. Marion had been outside all night, she hadn't gotten used to the cold, but watching the children shiver reminded her how high up in the mountains they were.

Herzog spoke to her a few times in German. Not knowing what they were saying made her uncomfortable. Herzog said something that sounded angry to her and turned back to Marion.

"She will stay quiet, she knows we are her best chance of survival. You can put the pistol away."

Marion shook her head. "I don't think so."

Alice watched them. She understood and spoke English. Marion still didn't trust her. Noah was right, your face didn't end up on those cards without you doing something bad. Marion wanted to ask her but didn't think she would be honest in front of the children.

"Alice? Right?"

The Nazi woman ignored her. "I'm Marion, I am new to this war stuff."

One of the boys had fallen asleep in her arms. The little girl cried softly. Alice rubbed her head passively. "Then what are you doing here?"

"Yeah, that is a heck of a story, my father was an expert in vampires."

"Was?"

"It killed him.  As soon as he is done with you krauts ..." Marion spun a wooden stake in her hand.

"Why did you bring that thing here?"

"The vampire? Come on Alice you're not that dumb. You know what your country has done."

Herzog shushed them. They both looked at him. He pointed at the sky. Marion thought it was thunder, but there was no flash of lighting. The low rumble was coming. The plane cut across the night toward them but was just far enough away that they could barely hear it. The officers couldn't hide anymore. If they wanted to escape, they would have to come out. It was the only reason Noah was allowing the first Nazi flight to land.

Marion watched Alice. She looked toward the manor. Somebody was still in there that she was worried about. Each second the plane got louder, any second now they would hear it inside. The final confrontation had begun.

# CHAPTER
# FORTY-SEVEN

HEINRICH LOOKED out the window that was on the south end of the library. He had it cracked and the cool breeze nipped at his skin. The torches at the airstrip had burned away. He didn't understand why they were still lit. He didn't know if the vampire was alone, or if the Allies had brought soldiers with him.

"He doesn't need anyone else," Himmler sat in Hitler's reading chair nursing a glass of American whiskey. He was reading his mind, or at least had guessed what he was wondering. Goring walked over with the bottle of whiskey and an empty glass. "Have a drink, Charles Lindbergh gave this bottle to the Fuhrer."

Heinrich shook his head. "He is not alone."

The vampire scratched at the door. He'd been making that awful sound almost every minute just to remind them that he was there. Heinrich looked at the clock and knew it was almost time. He opened the window wider and listened. The wind moved the trees, they rustled together. He heard it. The far-off sound of the plane engine.

"They're coming," he whispered.

Himmler finally downed the whiskey. Goring swigged straight from the bottle. They all looked at the door.

"I hear it too." The vampire called to them from the other side of the door. Goring pointed at Heinrich. "Maybe you can draw it off, and we can make it to the plane."

Heinrich went to Goring. "I'll draw it away, get the Fuhrer to safety."

"Wait!" Himmler snapped his fingers at Heinrich and waved him closer. He was unbuttoning his shirt. "Your uniform, quickly."

Sergeant Heinrich Hitzinger understood what he was asking. "My Fuhrer, that creature doesn't care about rank."

"You have your order Sergeant," Himmler held out his SS uniform.

Heinrich didn't move at first. The vampire scratched at the door. Outside the plane came closer. The two SS officers glared at him. He couldn't refuse, like it or not, this man was the Fuhrer. He unbuttoned as fast as he could. Himmler grabbed his uniform and Hitzinger held on to his IDs and papers. Himmler held out his hand.

"Sir? I..."

"When we get to the new Fatherland, you'll be the hero who saved the Reich." Goring patted his shoulder. He was worried about being captured and identified.

Sergeant Hitzinger buttoned up the SS uniform, it felt heavier than he ever remembered it being. He knew the rank labels were just symbols. When he fastened the top button, he turned and pointed his rifle at the window. The two SS officers covered their ears as he opened fire. The glass blew out and the wood and stone around it chipped away. Heinrich used the stock of the rifle to clear out a space to jump. He looked out, but he couldn't see the ground, he slung his rifle and planned to jump towards the tree hoping to would slow his fall. A true leap of faith.

"Come get me you fucking monster!"

Heinrich jumped and hit the tree spinning in the air. He fell longer than he expected and hit the ground with a brutal thud. He felt all the air in his body escape like it had been knocked out of his back. The ground was cold and unforgiving. He wasn't sure he could move again. He looked up and saw Goring looking out the broken window holding the candle. He wasn't sure that the man could see him, but he waved him off anyway. He hoped the vampire would assume they all went out the window.

He heard the sound of the plane roaring closer across the mountain. He tried to stand, but his whole body vibrated with pain. So here it was, the spot where he would die. Not the battles in Russia or the bunker under Berlin, but here on this mountain. Would the pain and cold get him or the monster?

*There you are.* They were not words but thunder bouncing around his skull.

He felt its approach in every single one of his aching bones. The monster was coming for him. He used the rifle as a crutch, found strength somehow, and pushed himself up. He imagined being with Alice again. He ignored the pain, as he had done so many times in Stalingrad. All those months without food or even ammunition. He pushed himself to his feet. Gritted his teeth and prepared himself to run.

There was a scream above. Heinrich turned and saw Goring's candle fall to the forest floor. He looked up and saw the vampire, it looked twenty feet tall as it came to the ground. In its hand was Goring's head. The vampire held it by the strands of hair he'd combed across hoping people wouldn't notice his hair loss. Part of Goring's spine dangled and dripped blood on the forest floor.

*Don't run!* Goring's voice echoed in his mind. But he had no vocal cords, so he knew whose voice was really speaking.

Heinrich did run. His body was like a flame, pain burned in every nerve ending. He heard the heavy footsteps of the creature and ran toward the light of the airstrip. He knew the creature was inside his mind because the footsteps behind him boomed with a familiar sound. The low thunder of bombs blanketing Berlin.

*Come back, Henri!* The voice was Alice. He knew better now.

*Daddy!* The voice of his daughter Karin. He heard his father and his mother, all of them calling on him to stop. To return to the manor. *No!* He kept running. He looked up into the sky and saw the blinking light. The plane got lower, closer each second;

he could almost see the shape of the BV 144. Its two engines roared even as the pilots cut the power for the descent.

He hoped that Alice and the children she saved were there waiting for the plane, it drove him to run through the pain, not the Fuhrer or the Reich, not the mocking of the creature. If he didn't survive, maybe the Fuhrer and Alice would. He felt some relief just seeing the plane in the sky. A group of German commandos that had been hiding came running toward the airstrip. He recognized a few of them from when they were lighting the torches. They cheered as the plane lowered in the sky.

Heinrich celebrated and pumped his fist. He turned around and didn't see the vampire. He only saw the men gathering around him. There were only a few left. He counted as quickly as he could. Nine men, that was all that remained. The plane roared as it came closer to them. Heinrich had to push the men to clear the strip.

They stopped at the edge of the airstrip and watched the plane as the roar of the engines got closer and louder. He felt a surge of pride. The world thought it had crushed Germany, that they were left for dead, but high above the world, they had come together to survive. The Jews had tried so hard to destroy them, bringing a devil himself to prey on them. His Alice would survive. His boy would be born and they would survive and build the new Fatherland. His son would return to Europe. Even if it took a hundred years, they would take Germany back.

He felt the warmth of the torches and walked past them to get to the spot where the trip wire would slow the plane to a stop. The plane was so close now he could see the glow of the torches on its bottom.

He looked down at the metal post that held the coil of the trip wire that would catch the back landing gear like a hook and slow the plane down. It was slack. It was supposed to be tight. Heinrich looked across the airstrip and saw a man holding bolt cutters and his heart sank.

It was a Jew. He could tell from across the airstrip. He was not in uniform, but his face was painted so he could easily hide at night. He didn't understand how he knew, he just understood that the man was Jewish. The Jew placed the bolt cutters on the trip wire and used all his strength. Heinrich wanted to shout no, but the snap of the wire froze him to his core.

The Jew dropped the dead tripwire onto the pavement and pointed his fingers like a pistol. He yelled to him before returning to the darkness. One word.

"Bang."

Heinrich turned to wave off the plane but it was too late. The back wheel hit the strip and at first the nine living German commandos jumped up and down with excitement. Heinrich fell to his knees. He put his hands on his face. He couldn't watch.

The plane roared as the air brakes caught and the tires hit the pavement. The air brakes couldn't handle it. The roar was so loud it was like having thunder in your bones. The mountain seemed to quake. Heinrich couldn't do it. He kept his eyes closed. He heard the cheers become screams.

There was not enough airstrip. The plane kept going back over the edge. When he finally opened his eyes, he saw it sink under the cliff. It was a long five, maybe ten seconds. The explosion would be heard down the mountain in Berchtesgaden. The flames rose up to reach for the moon and lit the night. A wave of heat passed over him. Not enough to burn him, but just enough that he felt it.

Heinrich watched one of the soldiers run to the edge to look over at the wreckage. From the distance, Heinrich could see the vampire coming up behind the soldier. He wanted to scream, to tell him *behind you*. It moved too fast. Heinrich didn't know what to do. It was over. The vampire held the soldier in the air before sending him down to the wreckage.

Heinrich remained on his knees, frozen in place, watching as the vampire attacked.

# CHAPTER
# FORTY-EIGHT

May 2nd 12:40 AM: The Eagle's Nest

THE PLANE WAS a few minutes early, but Noah had done his job. Mallory stopped on the front steps of the manor and turned around to see the flames coming up over the side of the hill. Might as well walk right in the front door. What few survivors were left had run to the plane expecting to be airlifted to safety. They might be coming back here so he wanted to move quickly. He taped a small flashlight to the barrel of his Baretta, he turned it on as he walked slowly through the open front door.

It was hard to believe he was here in the vacation home of Adolf Hitler. It looked like the last night of a war inside. Mallory held his breath because the smell was awful. Bodies torn to bits, soldiers who shat or pissed themselves in their last moments. He had heard the screams and sounds of chaos from outside, but seeing it was different. Reiter didn't mess around.

Mallory looked up the grand staircase and saw the Eagle's crest in broken stained glass. He assumed this was the way to the library. Mallory had to step over bodies, twice he stumbled on a Nazi that was not quite dead. The first reached for a pistol just beyond his fingertips. The second at the bottom of the stairwell even tried to grab his ankle but was too weak to grip him. The dying man begged, just saying "please," over and over. Mallory bent down closer and looked into the man's terror-filled eyes. On his shoulder was an SS rank. He knew the unit symbol Allgemeine SS. The unit in charge of maintaining racial purity. The men and women who maintained the camps.

He was a veteran of two wars, after the first one Mallory thought he was desensitized to it all. Nonetheless, liberating one of the death camps, or in his case, sneaking in and freeing one strategically important prisoner had been traumatic. Leaving that camp standing would haunt him at every last moment of his life. The sights and smells were something you never forget.

"Which camp?" Mallory tapped the Nazi's cheek with his pistol.

The Nazi just looked at him with a burning hatred. He didn't feel a shred of guilt, and neither did Mallory.

"Do me a favor lad, say hello to the Fuhrer for me." Mallory stood up. "In all due time."

Mallory heard the man crying still when he reached the top of the stairs. The second level was just as littered with corpses.

Logically, he knew the monster that did this was on his side but his heart still raced. He thought if any Nazis were left alive, they were probably sitting in puddles of tears or blood. The library door was open at the end of the hall. It took up the back half of the large manor. He saw a chair in pieces in the doorway. He stepped over it and saw the remains of a window that had been blown out with machine gun fire.

A body in an SS uniform hung over the edge of the window sill. When Mallory looked out over it towards the landing strip, he saw that the head was missing. Nazi blood poured down the side of the manor. Mallory grabbed the body's stiff legs and flipped it into the darkness. A few seconds later there was a thud. He spun the light to look at the shelves. There were hundreds of books, it was a library after all.

Alice in Wonderland. Pointing the light on the spines of the books at his eye level, he started by the door and scanned the titles. All the titles were in German, all expensive ancient books. He kept scanning until he got almost to the clock. It chimed for a quarter till one in the morning. Just beside the clock was one very large leather-bound volume.

*"Alice's Abenteuer im Wunderland."*

Mallory pulled on the book but something anchored it in place. He pulled harder and it worked as a lever. Gears turned and snapped as the clock rolled forward and turned on a track. It opened to reveal the next room. He went in and almost jumped when he saw a man sitting on the floor. The man put his hands up holding a cross. Mallory was more interested in the room, he shook his head.

It was as big as the library. Five desks were scattered around the room. Books were piled up and papers were everywhere. Two chalkboards were filled with math problems and equations. One board had a drawing of a rocket the height of a building. According to the reports, he was looking for one large leather briefcase that was meant to be taken to the new Fatherland with the most important top-secret Nazi research.

The balding man with wire-rim glasses wore an Infantry sergeant's uniform. He finally dropped the cross and pushed the briefcase under the desk behind him.

"Don't shoot!"

Mallory stepped closer and pointed the pistol and light at the man who cringed at the brightness.

"Sergeant, infantry." His English wasn't great.

Mallory took the pistol off him long enough to point his light at the board with the rocket.

"Big enough to destroy cities yeah." The German whispered.

Mallory aimed the gun back toward him. The light blinded the man again.

"Take me to America and the research is yours."

Mallory grinned. He was wearing an American uniform. "I ain't American mate. The truth is I don't want anyone having this shit. Not the Fuhrer's next of kin, not Uncle Sam or even Winnie."

"The British empire could rise again."

Mallory grinned "It could, but if you shitbags taught us anything, it's that empires are a load of bollocks,"

The Nazi sighed deeply. "I can help you, your country. I am a valuable…"

"Nah. If you are trying to appeal to my patriotic nature, tell me my boys will grow old and never have to kill a single German."

The man was not a Sergeant. He may have been a scientist, maybe an officer. That was one thing Mallory was certain of. He suspected if he had Noah's deck, his face would be a valuable card. Mallory stared longer; the Nazi put his hand over his face to block the light. Himmler. Mallory had never seen a picture of him without his hat, but this seemed most likely.

"Make it quick," Himmler said in German. Mallory thought about it. He would enjoy it but he felt like Reiter needed to work his magic on this one. Perhaps this was a fish for Noah's hook. Noah wanted him so badly.

"There is an American here leading the mission, he will want to make a deal, but he is Jewish and, as you can imagine, he is not in a merciful mood. Leave the case."

Mallory pointed the light towards the door built into the clock. Himmler cautiously got up and ran fast. Mallory waited until he knew he was gone.

Now that he was alone with the case, Mallory tried to work the latches. There were codes on each of the two locks. He angled the Baretta and with two quick angled shots blew the locks off. The leather case popped open.

There were several envelopes marked classified with Eagle's crests and swastikas on them. The first one he opened wasn't hard to figure out, even in German. Rockets six stories tall, built for going to space or transporting weapons, he wasn't sure. He saw enough flipping through it to know that these were plans for atomic weapons. *How close were they?* He didn't know.

The second envelope was filled with pictures of starving and dying Jews from one of the death camps. He saw the purple triangle on their striped uniforms. They weren't Jews but Jehovah's Witnesses. The pacifist sect was also gathered up. Their bodies were riddled with mutations, and boils. Their faces were a patchwork of various diseases. These were the test subjects for biological weapons.

The third envelope was the strangest of all. Pictures of SS officers, and wolves that stood like humans. The project was named WolfReich. Mallory wasn't too shocked considering they came to the mountain with a vampire. Hard to believe this kind of arms race was happening. He scanned the pages and found the location. A high mountain camp here in the Alps, one he never saw in any report. He took this envelope and folded it twice to hide it in his pocket.

He stuffed the rest back in the briefcase. He made up his mind, these papers would burn.

# CHAPTER
# FORTY-NINE

HEINRICH WAS SO stunned he froze. The burning plane created wreckage just over the cliff. The surviving commando unit moved to the edge. They all had weapons raised, and the two in the lead went right to the cliff. Out in the open, they were easy targets. He couldn't look away, not even blink. He wondered if the creature had compelled them with tricks into such a spot. The vampire ran past him and then floated in the air towards a commando at the cliff's edge, he turned and fired point-blank into the creature's chest. The bullets ripped through him, but nothing slowed him down. He kept going towards the screaming soldier. He threw him off the cliff as if batting a fly away from his face.

The vampire turned to face the raised rifle of the next commando. The machine-gun fire echoed around the mountains and had no effect on the creature. He toyed with them, knocked his machine gun away, and lifted the soldier in the air. The vampire roared before he dropped the man across his knees. The soldier screamed one last time as his spine snapped. One commando watched this close-up, he ran and jumped off the cliff. The vampire went to the edge to watch him fall.

Heinrich couldn't blame him. Two of the soldiers ran back the other way, the vampire pinned the first one and punched down, mashing the helmet into the ground. A skull couldn't survive that. Heinrich realized they were coming closer. The five remaining commandos screamed like children on a hayride.

He didn't want the creature to see him. He pushed up using his rifle and the fear overrode the pain that remained in his body. He moved into the tree line as fast as he could. The spell was broken, he listened but couldn't watch anymore. He ran as fast as his crushed back allowed.

Rational thought was long gone. "Alice!" He was scared to be found, but desperate to find Alice. If they could survive the night, just make it to dawn, they would be safe. "Alice!" His sweat soaked the smaller uniform that was fitted for the shorter Himmler. He spun around in the forest, desperate to find Alice. Maybe when she saw the plane crash, she was smart enough to return to the manor. He cursed himself for not coming up with a backup if the plane never came.

He made his way back to the manor. His eyes adjusted to the dark, and he moved faster as he got closer. It was lifeless, the moonlight lit it just enough to be seen. He heard screams in the distance. German men were still dying, he stopped and cursed his cowardice. That was the last of the men. It had to be. *Was he alone now?*

It had been some time since he heard a woman scream. That gave him hope that Alice might still be alive.

There was nothing he could do. He moved carefully around the base of the building, it was so dark he didn't even know he was under the window he'd jumped out of until his feet crunched on broken glass and he fell forward. He hit the ground and cursed; the pain surged again. When he turned over, he saw that it was a body that he'd tripped on. His boots soaked in a puddle of the man's blood, it took him a moment to realize that it was Goring's headless body.

Heinrich had seen such horror since his first campaign of the war. He rose through the ranks in part because he didn't complain. Plenty of soldiers complained about the conditions at Stalingrad, many thought the Fuhrer simply forgot to supply them. They used radio to issue commands so Heinrich knew there was no excuse. He understood certain indignities were the natural consequence of being a warrior. Berlin had not planned for a long Russian front. They assumed the brutality with which they handled the rest of Europe would work in Russia.

He had not been prepared for Russian brutality; no Germans were. They were a country that knew how to wage war. They excelled in cruelty and it was the days and nights on that front when Heinrich first questioned the wisdom of the thousand-year Reich. For that reason, he shot a Russian boy who pulled a cart with ammunition. He made the Italian farmer hiding the Jewish family pull them out of the basement himself. He made the farmer's family watch as he shot the Jews just because he didn't have a way to transport them. He believed the Fatherland was the greatest nation on earth, and that Aryan purity was the best fate for the future. No one else pulled those triggers.

The question haunted him now. *Would God forgive them for how they cleansed the earth?* This weapon, this creature was something beyond the horrors of war. With each passing moment, it felt like a judgment passed on their nation.

Survival seemed impossible. He'd recovered from that feeling before. He wasn't sure his mind could ever recover from this judgment. Above him, the clock chimed once for one o'clock in the morning. Now he was sure he was under the library and had a sense of where to go. The moon had moved enough to be on the far side of the trees. He was almost to the front of the large house. He heard the sounds of someone moving inside the manor. Light bounced around, electric, from a flashlight.

The vampire didn't need light. This was probably the bastard who unleashed the creature. The light shined out to the steps first. The person was being careful. Heinrich hid in the bushes and watched. He saw the pistol first. Short and stubby.

Heinrich almost let out an expression of shock. It wasn't a Russian soldier or a Smersh agent. The man wore an American uniform coming down the steps holding a leather briefcase in his other hand. Heinrich thought about attacking him but just watched him leave and go into the woods. Heinrich waited and watched to see if anyone followed him out. This man was so calm even as he left this house of horrors. The devastation he caused. It seemed the soldier was alone. This man, who brought this demon and unleashed it upon them.

Heinrich walked up the steps. He stopped at the door unsure if he could handle the horrors inside again. One thing he knew he couldn't handle was losing Alice. He walked through the door and prayed that Alice and the children were there.

He stepped inside and looked at all the bodies in the near darkness. They were a mess of organs, blood, and guts. He realized he would have to look through them in the morning to see if the new Fuhrer was among them.

"Alice?" Her name echoed back in the large empty manor. Silence. He thought about hiding in the basement. Maybe the armory, but he saw how much good weapons did. He would have to search the building for a cross, make a wooden stake...

"Here my love," her voice suddenly cut the silence. Heinrich's eyes followed the sound. He prayed but he was not answered.

There it was, larger than life at the top of the first floor landing, standing under the broken stained glass. He turned to look outside. *How could it be here so fast...*

RUN! Before the word passed through his mind, Heinrich fled.

He slammed the door shut. With it the thunderous echo of the slam and deeper darkness. Heinrich hit the door. Heinrich Hitzinger, a Sergeant in the German army. Personal protector of the Fuhrer and a three-time Iron Cross recipient closed his eyes and braced for death. *What good was yet another unanswered prayer?*

# CHAPTER
# FIFTY

<u>May 2nd 1:03 AM: The Eagle's Nest</u>

NOAH LOOKED across the flames of the torches along the airstrip and spotted Mallory. He stood on the pavement and held a briefcase. He held it closed but the locks were busted. They met in the middle of the paved strip where the black skid of the single landing gear had tried to brake.

"You found it," Noah raised an eyebrow.

Mallory dropped it on the pavement. "I'm burning it to ashes."

"Those are not *our* orders."

"Aye, sir."

"What are you saying, Mallory?" Noah leaned down to pick up the case.

"I'd spare myself the sight if I were you." Mallory used his leg to pull the case back.

"Don't lecture me on what the Nazis have done, I've seen the worst of it."

"I thought so too son, I really did, but this war is over." Mallory opened his lighter and the flame danced.

"Wait," Noah put his hands up. "The Japanese have not surrendered."

"You been inside the Nest yet?" Mallory pointed back at the building. "Have you seen what Reiter did up there?"

"Nazis, all of them."

"Yeah." Mallory nodded. "All this is their own doing, but it doesn't make it any less ugly."

Noah boiled over. "This is the wrath of God."

"You keep saying that," Mallory flipped his lighter onto the briefcase. Noah reached out and tried to catch it. Mallory grabbed his arm and pushed him back. "Let it burn, let it fucking burn."

"Goddamn it! Mallory!"

"That wrath spares no one."

Noah stared at the case as it burned. The rage boiled over. The faces from the camps, the bodies he found of those who died in hiding. The gaunt starving faces of Jewish children and all they endured. The filthy train cars, the broken families, and the tattoos with numbers that would never fade…

Noah unchained his rage and screamed. It echoed around the mountains. Mallory pulled him into a hug. Noah was shocked at first but fell into his old friend's arms. They had survived the war together Noah didn't know he needed this support until it happened.

"It's over," Mallory whispered. "You got em' Noah."

Noah let his head slump onto his friend's shoulder. The pain traveled through his body and escaped as tears through tightly shut eyes. The pain of the war shared between these men struck them both silent for an uncomfortable moment.

"Bastards," Noah whispered.

"They died knowing it, I promise you, Noah. They knew."

Noah pulled away from him and looked to the heavens. So many stars, so many nights he stared at the beauty of it while the world under it suffered. Noah closed his eyes. He prayed for healing. The words went through his mind in Hebrew but he was too moved to speak. They were gone, they did it. They stopped the demons from leaving. They prevented the Nazi flame from burning bright on new soil. Now they could end them forever.

Herzog walked with Alice Von Vogt and the children down the end of the runway. She was holding the oldest child's hand

and the younger ones were connected to her like a chain. Noah opened his eyes and just saw their shapes two hundred feet away.

"What did you do with Himmler?" Mallory asked.

Noah felt a rush of panic, like ice water flowing through his heart. He turned back to Mallory. "What? You saw him?"

Mallory knew he may have made a mistake. "Himmler, he was desperate to make a deal, I knew you wanted him personally. I told him to find the American Jew."

"He is still alive?" Noah turned back to Herzog and his group. It was then that he realized Marion was not with them. He and Mallory had the same thought. She was going after Reiter.

"Stay here," Noah pointed at Mallory.

He shook his head and started to follow. "Marion is my responsibility…"

Noah pointed at the burning briefcase. "You completed your mission." Noah held up the wooden stake. "Mine is still going, no monsters survive till dawn. Not one."

# CHAPTER
# FIFTY-ONE

May 2nd 1:05 AM: The Eagle's Nest

HEINRICH DIDN'T FEEL any remorse when he shot the boy in Stalingrad. Not one moment of shame or guilt. He knew he had crossed a threshold, but he had seen the five-year-old boy pulling the wagon every time on the mornings when the gunfire started up again. The wagon had bags of garbage, but that was by design. When the shooting started after the third day Heinrich knew how the Communists were getting their bullets. As Germans, they were rationing food and bullets. Already with orders to eat stale bread only in the morning and to shoot when they had a wide-open target.

He stopped the boy and dragged him from his cart and into the street. He needed a spot where the whole neighborhood could watch. He might have felt some kind of guilt with a full belly and some sleep. He didn't think about it again until he got his first Iron Cross. What he did, it had saved the lives of his men, and the incident confirmed to him that shame was just a weakness that could get him killed.

When he survived the battle of Stalingrad, he thought himself unkillable. Heinrich was nervous in the bunker, a part of him always thought he would find a way to survive.

With his face against the door of the Eagle's Nest, he closed his eyes and waited for death to overtake him. It took a creature so close to the devil himself to bring him here to this moment. For the first time, he honestly asked God to forgive him, to spare him death at the hands of a monster.

He heard footsteps coming closer.

"Please," Heinrich whispered. "Please."

"What?" The vampire spoke softly. He was right behind him. If Heinrich could crawl into the door he would. The creature sniffed him. His nose was so close to Heinrich's neck that it tickled, He felt the vampire open its jaws and put the fangs on his skin but it didn't bite. Like it was probing for a vein.

"Please…" Heinrich just wanted to see Alice again, to see his boy born. "Please…"

"You want mercy?" The vampire asked and disappeared. Heinrich felt a soft mist on the back of his neck. He was afraid to turn around even though he sensed the vampire was gone. He knew it was a trick. The cold mountain air was gone, he felt summer and thick humidity in the air. There was a day like this last summer in Northern Italy. The farmhouse was seared in his memory.

Heinrich opened his eyes and the Eagle's Nest had melted away. It wasn't just seeing the farmhouse, he felt it too. The memory overtook reality and Heinrich wished he knew how to resist this dark magic forcing him to relive it.

The Allies had invaded the southern region of Italy, and the battles were fierce. The Fuhrer sent them to assist the Italian units. The winter had been harsh on crops, and the summer was already uncomfortably hot. The farmer Mario Bastianini wanted only to manage his farm and avoid the war. He was desperate for money after the crop failure and had accepted a large sum of money to hide the Jews until summer when they were planning to go to the coast and catch a boat to Palestine.  With a failed olive crop and German forces looking for land to park their panzers, he cut a better deal.

Heinrich remembered this moment too well. He turned to see Bastianini pointing at the cellar door. He was powerless to stop himself. He was both in the moment and not. Both in his body and outside of it. The moment replayed like a runaway train.

Heinrich pulled out his pistol and waited for the farmer to open the cellar. The steps were wooden and flimsy, they were water damaged, and this basement flooded during storms. The smell of items that never fully dried hit his nose. When he got to the bottom of the stairs, he saw the Jews. Huddled in the corner he saw the father holding a young boy, the mother with two daughters, one under each arm. They cried, except for the mother. If she could use her eyes to kill this would be over.

"Please sir," The father didn't show any of his wife's anger, he only had fear. It was French he spoke but Heinrich understood. "Please have mercy."

This was complicated. The farmer had done the right thing but now Heinrich had a mess on his hands. It was natural for the rats, he remembered thinking. They could survive like this. He remembered thinking that maybe he should leave them be. The trains for deportation had to cross two mountain passes. For what? He knew their fate. It was mercy.

Heinrich raised the pistol and shot the mother first. Quick and painless straight through her skull. He couldn't stand to hear the pathetic father beg. He shot him next...

They weren't the first children Heinrich Hitzinger had killed. In his mind it was mercy. Reiter found plenty of horrible memories in the Nazi's mind. He truly believed it was an act of mercy. He believed deep in his cold heart that he was showing that family mercy. Reiter crawled back out of the Nazi's memory. He dragged Hitzinger back to reality with him, the man fell to his knees and the farmhouse was gone. Hitzinger, now back on the mountain, looked through tears up at Reiter.

"We were following orders, the racial purity of the Reich..."

Reiter held his long pale finger in front of his mouth and the soldier stopped speaking.

"I don't know if the world will accept the notion of your helplessness, but I do not." Reiter got closer to the Nazi. He felt his heart beat faster. "Unlike you, I am very aware that I became a monster. I am driven by an instinct I have grown to despise. That is why I was willing to sleep. That is the only death I was afforded. I saw this affliction as a curse, that is until you Nazis gave me a purpose. Something good I could do with this accursed power."

Reiter watched Heinrich's eyes. Even in the darkness of the manor, Heinrich could see the litter of bodies.

"You call this good?"

"You are the last black soul on this mountain, except the mother of your son. She too will pay but your child will eventually live. He will have to live with the curse of your blood. The poor Germans yet to be born."

Heinrich lowered his head.

"You never asked their names? I wondered, but I had only your memories to go by."

"What?" Heinrich was confused.

"The Jewish family at the farmhouse. You never even learned their names."

The Nazi turned his head to expose his neck. "Get it over with."

"I don't want your blood, you bastard."

Reiter reached into his chest and dug through his chest plate. For just a moment he showed Sergeant Hitzinger his own black heart. Heinrich watched it pump in the open air with the last moment of his life. The beating heart he was gifted by the universe. Reiter threw the heart on the floor before Hitzinger toppled over it in a heap.

Mission accomplished. Like clockwork he smelled another human, He didn't smell the woman until she crawled in the window. The freshly dead Nazi blocked the door. He turned slowly to see Marion Riverwood had entered the building and he knew she had a stake. The perfect one she needed. Forged on Romania soil and dipped in silver.

"And now my dear Marion, you believe it is time."

# CHAPTER
# FIFTY-TWO

MALLORY STOOD over the briefcase and watched the flames burn the papers inside. The leather of the case gave off an awful smell as it cooked. He knew Alice and the children were behind him. The children had been stunned into silence. Their best hope was to grow old and forget about this night. He could feel Alice watching him. Herzog kept his eye on her so Mallory could stare into the flames. It had been so long since he considered the idea that he could go home, that the war would ever end. He also knew if Brunner read the file folded in his pocket that he would end up chasing down more Nazi monsters. He still had choices to make. Most Nazis would assume the position and face judgment. Some wouldn't.

The full moon had crossed the sky and started the arc down into the horizon. He wondered if those creatures he read about in the file were running under this moon. Somewhere far off in another corner of the Fatherland, were they the last hope of the Germans?

"How are we getting off this mountain?" Alice asked in English. She must've thought Mallory was calling the shots. He kept his eyes on the fire.

"We didn't plan for that."

"Just come up here and unleash a monster on the Nazi bastards." Her voice laced with venom.

"Pretty much the plan," Mallory agreed."The roads are mined," she stated the obvious.

"We'll think about it when the job is done."

"You'll just go back to your lives," Alice said bitterly.

Mallory turned back to her. "Oh, I'm sorry did you want us to feel bad for you?"

He could see it on Alice's face, she wanted them to feel guilty. In her mind, the Nazis did the right thing and she had lost everything. She didn't say it but she still thought the Fuhrer was right. She still believed. He wanted her to understand something. He dug deep.

"There was a man who said goodbye to a wife and two boys back home..."

"Many Germans have said goodbye..."

"...This man had survived an earlier war as a young man. War for a husband and father is a different experience. That man that said goodbye and is gone. He will never return home."

"At least you have a home to return to."

"Lass," Mallory was close to spitting. "Not everyone on this mission agrees that you need to give birth to another one..."

Now she was keeping her mouth shut. Mallory didn't want to raise his voice, but the weight of the whole war bore down on him. All the missions, all the times he pulled a trigger, denoted a bomb or left someone to die. She had some nerve to speak this way. As if Germany didn't send their tanks into Poland.

"You want to live, keep those opinions to yourself. Don't give me a reason."

# CHAPTER
# FIFTY-THREE

<u>May 2nd 1:10 AM: The Eagle's Nest</u>

THE ROOM HAD TAKEN on an awful smell, some parts of the body were never meant to be exposed. More than one Nazi must have let their bowels go when faced with the monster. Marion stepped carefully over the bodies of the dead Nazis. She was positive she felt shit and guts squish under feet. She held her nose and stayed focused. He stood near the door, his back was to her but she understood that he was very aware of her presence.

"And now my dear you believe it is time."

Reiter reached out to her mind, she felt invisible hands reaching for her. Even with him in front of her, she felt surrounded. She lifted the large silver cross, it had belonged to her father. The hands retreated, but Reiter turned and smiled at her. He didn't hiss or run from it. His eyes seemed to glow as they stared at each other.

"He was holding that very cross when he died."

"When you killed him?"

He shook his head. "Mallory has allowed you to think that so you would stay angry and focused."

"You killed my father."

"Professor Riverwood had a bad heart; he saw the fuel of his nightmares in front of his eyes. In that sense yes, I killed him."

The Nazis had kidnapped her father and brought him to Europe. He survived the stress of that but not confronting Reiter. He killed all the Nazis that night in his castle, she had no reason to believe anything else about the night Reiter woke after centuries of slumber. She wasn't sure how much he understood about what was happening.

"I think you killed him just like the others."

"Like the Nazis?" Reiter waved at the bodies. "Hardly. Your father, I didn't mind him. He had so much he wanted to ask. You know that. He spent more time thinking about me than he ever did you or your poor mother."

Marion raised the cross higher. "No more mind games. No monsters live till dawn."

"Such a waste Noah, look at what I did? What I can do still."

Noah? Marion didn't see him come in. Where? She was afraid this was a trick to get her to look away. Noah walked slowly out of the darkness holding the wooden stake ready to attack.

"The job is not done. Himmler is still alive."

Reiter shook his head. "He was never here. Every last Nazi soul has been destroyed I promise you that."

"Mallory saw him. He talked to Himmler. He was here."

"Yes, I understand the Nazis all thought he was here but I never felt his presence, not on this mountain."

"The mission is not over," Noah insisted.

"She thinks it is, and me with it." Reiter smiled and pointed to Marion.

"We can't let you live Reiter, you're a parasite." Marion stepped closer, holding the cross out as far as her arm would extend. "I can't live with that."

Reiter reached up and knocked the cross out of her hand. "There is no god to punish me."

Marion lifted the stake, Reiter grabbed her arm and held it. "You can die you bastard!"

Noah didn't move. Marion looked at him, silently begging him to help her, to do something, anything.

"Do you know how many times I could kill you all?"

Marion tried to push the stake closer, but Reiter was too strong. He tossed her across the room, she landed against a dead Nazi with a thud. Noah didn't move closer, not even to help her up. She felt like screaming. She reached into the bloody pile of dead Nazis looking for the stake she had dropped. It was gone. She now had to hope that Noah did the right thing.

The problem was, this is exactly what Noah wanted. Justice as fast as possible, no trials, no excuses. It was a bloodbath, they had unleashed a monster and now that she saw what he could do, she knew he was right. He gave himself up and he played the game.

They all knew there would be Nazis who would still run and hide. This country was crawling with guilty monsters with plenty to hide.

"I'm cursed Noah," Reiter ignored her. His tone was different, the playfulness was gone. "I am a prisoner with desires so deep you cannot imagine."

"What are you saying, Reiter?"

"For the first time in centuries, I did a good thing, yes?"

Marion lay in a pile of bodies and wondered if that could be true. Could this be justified? The fact that they did this.

Noah nodded. "You did good tonight."

"Put down the stake, and I promise you I will get every last Nazi I can."

Marion shook her head. "No! Don't."

Noah walked over to Marion and offered her a hand. She watched the creature relax. Marion looked into Noah's eyes as he helped her up.

"Not this way," Marion whispered.

This time she was closer and saw the hurt in the man's eyes. The pain of the things he'd seen and lived through. He didn't have to explain himself. She wouldn't argue.

"We're a team now," Noah whispered. She saw Reiter nod. She looked away. Marion lifted herself up and walked toward Reiter standing at the front door. She looked at the vampire and she didn't feel him using any of his powers toward her.

"Not me," Marion looked around at the carnage. "The war is over for me."

Marion walked out into the night. Mallory was there, he held his Baretta at his side.

"He is still alive?" Mallory asked.

She nodded. "If you can call that alive."

"He is Noah's problem now. We completed our mission."

"Not mine Greg."

"Oh Lass, weapons like Reiter...You can't destroy them."

Marion hugged her friend. "I want to go home."

Mallory rested his head against hers. "We are. We're going home."

# CHAPTER
# FIFTY-FOUR

<u>May 2nd 5:25 AM: Bottom of the Mountain</u>

HE BREATHED a deep sigh of relief when he saw the first purple glow of the sunrise. It signaled salvation. For hours he marched along the road, positive at any moment the darkness would come alive and take him. When the sun finally lit the whole sky a soft blue and the stars faded, Heinrich Himmler cried tears of joy.

He survived. He stopped, took off his glasses and let the sun warm his face.

It was impossible in these moments not to reflect on his journey. There was a time in his life when he spent three weeks alone trying to mix and match different breeds of wheat seeds. Would that student recognize the man he had become? It was a race to be ready, to prove himself. The farm was just a two-hour drive north of Technische Hochschule in Munich. The school gave him a train ticket but he had to walk the last two miles from the station. He arrived at the farm just minutes before a big downpour. He had to take a few breaks on that walk to let his arm rest. He only brought a few outfits to wear in the fields, so they fit nicely in his backpack. It was the other case with the wheat seeds that felt heavy as bricks.

The wheat farmer was happy to see him, after two summers of reduced yield he needed help. Heinrich Himmler was never told the Farmer's name before he left. Benjamin Sternberg, A joke or lesson he wasn't sure. No one at the university told him that the farmer was a Jew. He had been vocal on campus about the Jewish problem. Attended the rallies protesting the Treaty of Versailles. There was only one Jewish professor in the agronomy department. Plenty on campus in other schools. He was positive this was a cruel joke, as he was outspoken about any and all opinions he held. But his wheat research was too important to his career. He couldn't pass on the internship.

Sternberg of course couldn't be bothered to spend a drop of petrol going to pick up his intern. He invited Himmler to dine with his family from time to time and offered to treat him like a part of the family operation. But the relationship was always cold, everything on this farm was about the bottom line. Himmler watched him take government funds, work his interns and then charge raised rates at the exchange. One night Himmler watched Sternberg and his son making a list of the multiple jobs he and the other interns were expected to do. The father had a saying he was fond of, he said it whenever he piled more work on him. *Frankly son, two birds is not enough for my stones.*

Heinrich heard him say it more times than he could count.

He had a promising career in agronomy until one night changed the direction of his life. November 8th, 1923. There had been marches before, but that night they got the attention of the nation. The so-called Beer Hall Putsch, it was called an insurrection but they were as surprised as anyone. Hitler was a more powerful leader than they believed. Jail was the best thing that could have happened to their revolution. Hitler wrote his book behind bars, but Himmler was free. He tried to move on with his life. He was questioned by the police many times. Everyone knew he was there. Rumors spread.

Now as he walked along the muddy path heading down the mountain, he thought about the shame he felt. Twice he had sat in interviews across from Jews. Disgusted that he had put on his finest and had to ask them for a job, but he did. Aryan, Jew, or some half-breed, all the interviews ended the same way. They would ask him if he was there at the march in Munich. When they didn't ask, he would nervously wait for the subject to come up and he looked defensive in meetings. They knew who he was. No matter how many times he said it would not affect his performance, it did. *They never hired him.*

Farms and all the production industry around it needed government welfare to operate. The cowards were afraid to hire him after that. He lost his apartment and had to move back in with his parents. It was a family shame. *Had one farm or food producer hired him, would history have played out differently?*

He had no choice. When Hitler got out of prison, he worked harder to get into office by legal means. Heinrich Himmler had nothing else, he had to join those efforts. He left the church, breaking his mother's heart. He worked to make her proud of his activism. He started as a propaganda minister, handing out leaflets on the street. The early years were about the message, and then when the power came it was almost a shock that they were given the nation and the ability to make their thousand-year Reich a reality. When he and Goring had drinks, they would admit they never believed it would really happen. Hitler's dream was something they were comfortable demanding, but never believing it would actually happen. It was hard not to believe they were chosen. When it happened, it was impossible not to believe God had chosen them.

He always had that in his mind when he made the hard decisions. He looked back up at the Eagle's Nest. The dawn was just now lighting the tip of the mountain. He remembered a night when the Fuhrer and several leaders of the party drank long into the night. It was August of '41. He had just returned from a trip to the front in Minsk. He attended the execution of one hundred Jews. The experience left him feeling sick to his stomach. He watched the pain on his SS officers' faces as they performed the deed. He couldn't put them through that again, the act of shooting so many prisoners was traumatic for his men.

Ten million Jews populated Europe alone and the Reich would never survive if the Jews, Gypsies, and Communists were allowed to weaken their empire from within. He couldn't see his men surviving the act of putting down a million Jews one at a time, let alone the rest. He had a train ride from the front to think about it. Sternberg was a decent man; he thought about him and his family. They were kind enough, but God had put Himmler in this position to make tough decisions. They all knew a Jew here or there that meant well, but if they let even one remain to sabotage the future then they would be right back where they were in 1916.

*I have a better way.* He promised the Fuhrer. Four months of planning led to a meeting he held on January 20th just outside of Berlin. *Work: back-breaking, brutal work.* They needed everyone at the front and the Jews would just have to work. They needed ammunition made, and tanks and planes would not make themselves. They would make them and no one needed to be concerned about their safety. Those unable to work or dangerous individuals would meet the gas as a group. The next summer when he first toured the camp, it was a great relief to him how much easier and more controlled the process was compared to what he saw in Belarus.

On a morning like this, after all he had seen, walking all night to get away from the monster he wanted to tell himself that he never had a choice. If he hadn't done what he did, the war would have been bloodier, and the pain even deeper. This night felt like the night of the Putsch. The feeling of that high, the empowerment they felt when they took to the streets, followed by the crushing defeat of the trials and those many painful job interviews. From returning home to live with his mother to becoming the architect of the final solution.

A few hours ago, he was the Fuhrer awaiting a flight to start his own nation. Now the Jews had won. Germany was crushed, the last hope of the Reich slaughtered in a bloodbath.

He walked all night off the road to avoid mines, his boots were filthy, his pants urine-soaked, at some point facing Reiter, he lost control. He could see the smokestacks of Berchtesgaden across the lake and he could almost smell the bread baking. He dreamed of the food he would eat. He knew he just needed to get out of Germany somehow. They would be looking for SS officers. Commanders, not enlisted men. He reached into his pocket and for the first time in the sunlight, he looked at the ID.

Heinrich Hitzinger.

The man's uniform was a little big on him, but it was an infantry uniform. The same first name was not ideal but a shave and a few scratches on the picture would have to do. For now, he had only one goal. Escape Germany.

# CHAPTER
# FIFTY-FIVE

<u>May 23nd 4:25 PM: British 31st Civilian Interrogation Camp</u>
<u>near Lüneburg</u>

NOAH HAD DRIVEN for two hours across the German countryside as fast as he could when he got the news. The camp was near the northern city of Luneburg, it was smaller than the American camp he came from. The Germans fleeing north had no idea the Royal Navy had blockaded the northern ports, although a few ships got through. The border to Denmark was swarming with checkpoints.

This camp was built to connect to the former police station and was surrounded by barbed wire fences. High-value prisoners were taken inside and destined for transfer to Nuremberg where the trials were set to begin as soon as possible. Years earlier, Stalin had demanded several million workers to rebuild their country, but France wanted workers too. The Germans' faces told him that reparations were being explained to them.

Armed British rangers watched everything from the towers. An orderly line of Germans waited to be interviewed. Very few were in uniform, all were going to claim that they were hardly involved in the war, following orders, or that they merely pushed pencils. He had been all over the country visiting these camps, his deck of cards handy, although at this point all the camp interrogators had their own decks.

Mallory waited for Noah on the bench near an open parking space next to a row of trucks. Noah grinned and was happy to see his friend back in his British uniform. They had not spoken since the Easy Company and a full squad of Paratroopers came to clean up their mess. Their mission was classified, after General Patrick and Field Marshal Brunner's hand-picked clean-up crew whisked away the bodies and even did some repairs. There was no evidence of a bloodbath. Noah left before the crews arrived but the rest of the team waited.

They all felt good about the mission. For Noah, there were only two open wounds, two failures of the mission in his mind. The biggest was the man in the wire-rimmed glasses. Noah stepped out of the Jeep. It had been a foggy morning with clouds that rolled east toward them from the North Sea. The late afternoon was clear, the sun was warm as summer had almost arrived. Mallory put out his hand but Noah pulled him into a hug and patted his back hard.

"Look what the cat dragged in." Mallory laughed and smiled at his friend. It had been three weeks and a day but it felt like a thousand years had passed. The unconditional surrender was just reached. The soldiers had already celebrated and spent much of the afternoon taunting the Germans. A large part of Noah hoped no deal would ever be reached.

"Sorry, I left so quickly."

"You had your reasons." Mallory had thoughts he chose to keep to himself.

"I saw the photos of Easy Company; you drink any of the Fuhrer's beers?"

"You're damn right," Mallory grinned. "It was quite the party, and no one had any idea what happened in those walls."

"Good for them," Noah was afraid to ask, but it was the other open wound. "Alice and the kids?"

"The little ones went to family somewhere, Alice went to an interrogation camp near Munich, but I suspect you know that."

"We were there, she walked out. Said she was a nurse in Munich. They believed her and just let her walk out."

"We?" Mallory's glare went to the coffin tied down in the back of the Jeep.

No point in denial, Noah nodded. Mallory understood what was in the coffin. There was a stamp with fake dog tag numbers for a soldier with an address in Alabama. He was driving a casket all over the country but since the war was ending, no one seemed to notice.

"If you're here then I assume you got my telegram then."

"You knew I was coming or you wouldn't have been sitting here, you sure it is him?" Noah pulled out the deck of cards.

"Put it away lad, it is him. You have your royal flush."

Noah walked across the camp and Mallory followed him as they talked.

"Surprised he didn't take a pill."

"I believe he tried, but the interrogators have them now."

"So he can what? Face trial? Explain why he did it? Fuck that."

"We couldn't find you at first Noah, if only you had been here earlier. We have strict rules for how we have to treat the buggers now that there is peace."

Noah stopped him. "Can you get me in there or not?"

"You can't kill him, Noah. Not in that room, not now."

"You have my word I will not touch him."

"You swear on the…"

"Yes, Greg. I swear on the Torah, on my mother's kugel recipe, you name it I'll swear by it. Not one hand on him."

Mallory looked up at the sky it was still a few hours until the sun went down. They both knew what he was thinking.

"Just me, we'll just chat a little."

They walked slowly through the camp. It was like a maze of tents, barbed wire, and hastily constructed fences until they got to the Luneburg police station. A 31st British interrogation sign was nailed to the wall. Mallory handed papers to the guards who waited at the door.

"The captain is waiting for you." They waved Noah in and he was confused that Mallory didn't follow him.

"Brunner has given you a green light to go in, but I have another mission. A hold-out camp in Poland, they have some nasties I have to take care of."

"Nasties?"

"You might be the only person who believes me. Even a man who is pure of heart and says his prayers at night...well you know the rest."

"You need us?"

"I sure hope not."

They shared one last hug. Noah was surprised at first at how long the man squeezed him. When he stepped back Mallory gave him a smile.

"Next time you're in London, the pub is on me."

Noah nodded and walked carefully into the building, an officer in his uniform with a captain's rank shoulder saluted him. Noah waved it off. He had no rank but he suspected that Field Marshal Brunner made it seem as though he did. If they followed his orders, that was good.

"Captain Thomas Selvester, nice to meet you, sir." He shook Noah's hand with a firm grip. "The prisoner and two aides were captured at Bremervörde. His ID says Hitzinger but it's him for sure."

Selvester handed Noah the Hitzinger ID. "He insists that is his name, this is the third camp." The British captain held up a bandaged hand. "He figured out this morning that we knew him. I had to fish a pill out of his mouth. He still had another one."

Noah understood. "Thank you Captain I would like some time alone with the prisoner."

Two guards were posted outside the door. Selvester would wait, that was fine. It was his prisoner, Noah understood. Noah started inside the room but the captain cleared his throat and put out his hand. Noah sighed and unclipped his holster and handed the pistol over.

"You can't kill the bastard I'm afraid."

"Is there a window in there?"

"A small one covered by bars, he can't get out."

Noah nodded. "I was just hoping for little natural light." They opened the door and he took a breath before stepping inside. Noah felt sweat forming under his collar just looking at him. For the duration of the war, this was the single most vile man on his wish list. Here he was. Hands and feet handcuffed.

On the table just beyond his reach was a white pill. Noah appreciated what a mean son of bitch Captain Selvester was being. Leaving Himmler's cyanide pill there for him to look at and think about.

Himmler looked up at him and at that moment Noah felt the recognition. If Himmler had the strength to break the chains and run, he would've. Noah wasn't sure if Himmler knew he was there that night at the Eagle's Nest but his reputation for revenge was well known.

"I don't think I need to introduce myself, do I?"

Noah looked at the small window near the ceiling, it let in the late afternoon sun. Designed to naturally light the room. Perfect.

"You had a nickname for me, you remember?"

Himmler didn't say anything.

"It's fine because I remember. Pardon me but my German is not great. Die furchterregende Ratte. Don't worry I kinda like it actually."

Noah nods, and Himmler looks down at the pill. The only escape he has left.

"I bet you really, really want that pill." Noah spun it once on the table. "As you may have heard the surrender is official. The British and American governments want you to stand trial but we have unfinished business."

"My name is Sergeant Heinrich Hitzinger, I don't know you or what you are talking about."

"Well, Sarge I have good news for you."

Himmler was confused.

"Congratulations, you're going to be a father."

Noah dropped the Hitzinger ID papers on the table. "We let Alice and the children walk away from the Eagle's Nest. Alice Van Vogt, you remember the Fuhrer's typist. The one having your baby."

Himmler's jaw lowered slightly. This was a different kind of speechless. Terror creeped in.

"That's right," Noah pointed at his chest. "I was there at the Eagle's Nest. I am one hundred percent the man behind the power of God you experienced."

Himmler looked up at the fading sunlight in the window.

"And yes, it is getting dark Mister Himmler."

His breath increased, sweat formed under his arms and leaked from his temple.

"I'll cooperate, whatever you need, testify against whoever, just don't let that thing in here."

Noah nodded and he looked at his watch. "We have the time, it is almost summer you know, longer days."

"Please, don't, just listen."

"Heinrich please," Noah reached up and pushed the wire-rim glasses back up the ridge of his nose. "You know Reiter, I mean your people tried to take his castle from him. He and I have talked about it and at first we couldn't understand how you escaped."

Himmler closed his eyes.

"Yeah, I wouldn't want to hear this either. You see Reiter could smell your blood, but he has a way of reading souls. That is how he gets into our minds to exploit our guilt and fears. They are like doors into the soul, people open up for him. You just don't have one, asshole. That is the only explanation we could think of. I think you were born with one, but somewhere, somehow you lost it. Not even a rotten soul, just nothing."

"Give me the pill you rat," Himmler whispered. He looked Noah in the eye. "I did it, so many Jews I killed them slowly. I invented the gas…"

Noah shook his head and held up his hand. "I think we'll just wait for the sun to go down."

Himmler looked away, ugly huge tears came, as the terror washed over him. Noah thought maybe Reiter had found his mind and wormed into his soul, but it was the horrors of the man's life and the memory of the creature that hunted him down. He looked at the darkening sky one more time and seized. His heart pumped faster than his chest could handle.

"How does it feel to know in a century your crimes will still be remembered?"

Himmler was dying, so filled with fear, his heart nearly pounded out of his chest. Noah pushed the pill closer. Close enough he didn't need hands. He stood up and left the Reichfuhrer to die alone.

# EPILOGUE

SOMETHING HIT HER BEDROOM WINDOW. It was enough to wake her. Karin looked at the window as a small crack spider-webbed into a network of cracks. It took too much effort, but she sat up and dropped her ancient legs to the floor. A three-week-old episode of the *Price is Right* droned away. The TV lit her veiny legs and the wrinkled feet that made her feel a thousand years old. She should go back to bed, but her throat was so dry. The grandchildren would be here in the morning, they loved their Oma, even if Martin and Tracy never wanted to bring them.

Martin was a blessing and a curse. They didn't get along, and they had fought her whole life. She could never explain it to him, but he was the spitting image of his father. A man she tried so hard to forget.

From her bedroom window, you could see the glow of New York City. She had lived this close to it for forty years but rarely made it through the tunnel. Even all those years when Martin lived in the city, he rarely came to see her. He never invited her to their home in Queens. She worked typing up ledgers for Patterson Insurance as long as they let her. She worked overtime during filing season or whenever available. She did everything she could to keep her childhood a secret.

Martin resented that she changed the subject whenever he asked questions about his father, her parents, or growing up in the old country. She hid her accent, but when she was tired or angry, she slipped. Sometimes spoke German in her sleep according to Martin. She stopped falling asleep on the couch after that.

Once Martin left for NYU, she just spent her evenings watching television and hoping it kept the memories away. She liked the Westerns in the 60s and now her favorite show was *St. Elsewhere*. She taped *Price is Right* on the VCR, and it was the last thing she watched nightly. She was normally asleep by the showcase showdown. Sometimes she rewound, but sometimes she just taped over them.

She knew she was seventy-three years old, but looking at her faint reflection in the window she saw a gaunt and frail old woman she couldn't understand. All-purpose had left her when Martin left home.

She needed a drink of water. Stumbling into the kitchen, she heard Bob Barker in the other room tell the contestant to spin again. It was a short hallway but it was dark. For years after Martin had grown up, she kept his faint night light plugged into the hallway. Reagan was president when it burned out, and still, it sat there in the plug.

She flipped the switch for the kitchen light. One medium-sized cockroach ran to hide under the fridge. It was easy to erase the past when it was so far away. That is why she never allowed questions. She told Martin the same thing so many times. *You are here, I am here. You are loved and your belly is full. You don't need to know.*

She looked at the time. The time on the microwave said 12:23. It was Sunday now. She grabbed a pen to X out Saturday on her calendar. Her 1989 New Jersey Bird Watcher's calendar was a part of her morning routine, but she had forgotten to cross out the days since Wednesday. She took the sharpie to Thursday, Friday, and Saturday but stared at that last day in April.

She stared at the box on the calendar for a long moment. Just another day she told herself. The sound of that pistol booming in the next room echoed across forty-four years. A new name, a new life. No one knew who she was but it was days like these as summer approached when memories became like a raw exposed nerve.

*No one knows,* she told herself.

Smash. Karin turned to the front door. There were two small windows the width of a book that stretched the height of each side of the door. The right window was shattered and a hammer was breaking it away. She ran to the front door and the glass shattered over her. She fell back and saw an arm reach into the door and flip the deadbolt.

It took her a second try, but she got up and hobbled back into the kitchen. She stopped when she saw the shape of an impossibly tall man blocking the light. The door opened behind her. An older man stepped in the door. He was wearing a sweater, his undershirt held back a belly that poked out under it. His hair was gone on top, what grey hair he had on the sides and back of his head was wildly unkempt. He held a wooden baseball bat. A word was carved into the bat. Tzedakah.

"Hello Alice," The old man nodded.

Karin turned back to her kitchen and wasn't Karin anymore. For the first time in decades, she was Alice Van Vogt again. The tall figure came into the light, she shouldn't have been shocked. Forty-four years and she always thought he would find her. Reiter towered over her. He smiled at her; his beautiful Romanian features had not aged a day. His skin was still the color of milk but it made the nightmare feel even less real. There was a part of her that could forget Alice, after Martin left it was easier.

She shook her head. "I'm Karin Towns I was born in New Jersey."

"It is her," Reiter sniffed the air but that was for show because he was in her mind.

The old man leaned on his bat like a cane. He reached into his pocket and pulled out something. A playing card with a picture on it.

Alice closed her eyes. She didn't have to look, she knew the beautiful young face. It was another lifetime, one that seemed impossible now. The Fuhrer's orders. *Get a photo for your parents in Munich.* She had bitten her tongue so many times. She hated watching the way the media portrayed her Fuhrer. She remembered his kindness to her. The sweet way he treated Eva, and Blondie the dog dutifully curled up at his feet when they worked.

She was the woman who typed his speeches, but she was more than that. She typed up orders and communications with the front lines and camps. He had trusted her with the darkest secrets of the Reich. *One day my dear the Jew will be nothing but a memory, a story you tell your children to scare them.*

"You let me live," she whispered. Alice knew now, this old man was Noah Samvovich. OSS operative during the war and thought to be dead. It was him. She was positive.

"We let your child live." Noah walked over to the picture on the fireplace taken at his high school graduation. "He looks like Hitzinger, dead ringer."

"You've grown old Noah. You still have hate in your heart."

The old man cleared his throat. "Call it by whatever name you like but Martin lives, Germany lives on. The Jews, we live on despite what you and your people…"

"We were trying to save Europe, I begged for scraps with my father on the streets in 1916, you think you alone suffered?"

"I don't have time to listen to this. Do you?" Reiter grabbed her by her shirt. She looked defiantly at them.

"He was a good man," Alice looked at Noah. In her anger she decided to say she would let go of her truth, her feelings she'd buried for forty-four years just for survival. "He was right, you poisoned Europe and now it is just a collection of socialist states letting any vermin in no matter what race…"

She felt Reiter crawling into her mind. He stopped her from speaking. It was like he put a clamp on her brain.

"There she is, how many execution orders did you type for him? How many speeches did you type that called for an end to my people?" Noah stepped back. "You are the last one Alice. You were well hidden, I'll give you that." Noah signaled Reiter and walked out. He didn't get pleasure in watching.

———

Noah heard Alice's last scream. He stepped out into the night; it had been a warm day but the air temperature had dropped fifteen degrees. He zipped up his jacket. This Jersey City neighborhood stayed dark, no one investigated the scream. He saw the glow of city lights, just across the water was the city that never sleeps. The glow was so strong there were no stars to see.

It felt like a miracle, the idea that the war could end for him. Forty-four years and it never felt over. Thanks to the Ratlines there were Eichmanns and Heims all over Central and South America. So, they worked on their Spanish.

The front door opened. Reiter stood behind him. Plenty of places they could celebrate, but this was not that kind of evening. At the end of this road was always a cliff, never an oasis. They had no lives except hunting and killing Nazis.

Noah pointed to the truck and the casket that they had used whenever they were stateside.

Reiter shook his head. Noah understood but hoped he would change his mind. This was the last one, and the most important to them. The one that had slipped through their fingers.

"Why not just sleep?"

"I have experienced thousands of lives Noah, taken more. I know you can live with this, but I can't. Not anymore."

"So, what do we do?" Noah asked.

Reiter was now his oldest friend. Even if he wasn't human, he smiled at him. "Just stay and watch the sunrise with me."

Noah nodded.

"What will *you* do my old friend?"

He had never considered it. Noah couldn't remember the boy that left for the war. The first time he found a family dead, hiding in an attic, killed by summer heat. Out of desperation to not be found by the Nazis they had suffocated. Noah had devoted his every breath to justice. He ran his fingers along the etching on the bat.

Tzedakah.

He threw the bat into the tall grass in the yard. That was the only answer he could give. If Reiter was that interested in his confusion, he could read his mind. Noah knew he would wrestle with it but the hardest part was he had no family or loved ones to throw the dirt on him when he arrived back at Sons of Jacob in St. Paul. When he is buried next to his mother the Rabbi will dutifully perform the rituals and follow traditions as laid out in his will, but to him, it will just be another man.

"You're a hero Noah," Reiter whispered. "No one else has to know."

"Hey Count, get the fuck out of my head OK?"

They laughed for one last time. In silence, they sat until the sky grew purple. Noah heard his skin burning before the sun poked over the horizon. It was quick, as the rays of sunshine hit the porch, Count Reiter, across an ocean from his native land, kept his eyes wide open. For the first time in four hundred years, he watched the sunrise.  His mission accomplished, he became dust.

# ACKNOWLEDGMENTS

First, I want to thank Ivan Zoric, it was late after a Portland Trailblazers game and we were talking hoops over text and it turned to movies. At some point Ivan said "Any movie could be better if you add a vampire." Before I went to bed, I had the concept and the title. Leza and Christoph at CLASH, it was important to me to publish with members of the tribe and I knew Christoph would get it. Laina Cohn for helping navigate the Hollywood stuff, my writing collaborators Anthony Trevino, Edward Morris, and Langhorne. Josh Trank—the project didn't go forward but working with you just before writing this was a huge influence on the structure of this story. I can't thank you enough. Devlin McCarthy for reading an early draft for historical accuracy, Desmond Reddick was the first reader. Cari for of course dealing with me putting in 12 hours days on this one.

# ABOUT THE AUTHOR

David Agranoff is a novelist, screenwriter and a Horror and Science Fiction critic. He is the Splatterpunk and Wonderland book award nominated author of 10 books including the novels the Cli-fi novel *Ring of Fire*, *Punk Rock Ghost Story* and the science fiction novel *Goddamn Killing Machines* also from CLASH. He co-wrote a novel *Nightmare City* (with Anthony Trevino) that he likes to pitch as The Wire if Clive Barker and Philip K Dick were on the writing staff. As a critic he has written more than a thousand book reviews on his blog *Postcards from a Dying World* which has recently become a podcast, featuring interviews with award-winning and bestselling authors such Stephen Graham Jones, Paul Tremblay, Alma Katsu and Josh Malerman. For the last four years David has co-hosted the Dickheads podcast, a deep-dive into the work of Philip K. Dick reviewing his novels and the history of Science Fiction. His non-fiction essays have appeared on Tor.com, NeoText and Cemetery Dance. He roots for the Portland Trailblazers and Indiana Hoosiers Basketball. He lives in San Diego.

# ALSO BY CLASH BOOKS

**HEXIS**
Charlene Elsby

**EVERYTHING THE DARKNESS EATS**
Eric LaRocca

**THE BLACK TREE ATOP THE HILL**
Karla Yvette

**I DIED TOO, BUT THEY HAVEN'T BURIED ME YET**
Ross Jeffery

**CHARCOAL**
Garrett Cook

**THE LONGEST SUMMER**
Alexandrine Ogundimu

**ANYBODY HOME?**
Michael J. Seidlinger

**PEST**
Michael Cisco

**LES FEMMES GROTESQUES**
Victoria Dalpe

**THE PAIN EATER**
Kyle Muntz

**THE ECSTASY OF AGONY**
Wrath James White

**WE PUT THE LIT IN LITERARY**

CLASHBOOKS.COM

FOLLOW US

TWITTER
IG
FB

@clashbooks

Printed in the USA
CPSIA information can be obtained
at www.ICGtesting.com
JSHW021930100823
46328JS00001B/1